SURRENDER

SURRENDER

RAY LORIGA

Translated from the Spanish by
Carolina De Robertis

A Mariner Original
Houghton Mifflin Harcourt
BOSTON   NEW YORK
2020

First Mariner Books edition 2020

hmhbooks.com

Library of Congress Cataloging-in-Publication Data
Names: Loriga, Ray, 1967– author. | De Robertis, Carolina, translator.
Title: Surrender / Ray Loriga ; translated from the Spanish by Carolina
De Robertis. Other titles: Rendición. English
Description: First Mariner Books edition. |
Boston : Houghton Mifflin Harcourt, 2020.
Identifiers: LCCN 2019024026 (print) | LCCN 2019024027 (ebook) |
ISBN 9781328528520 (trade paperback) | ISBN 9781328529916 (ebook) |
ISBN 9780358172345 (eISBN) | ISBN 9780358298724 (eISBN)
Classification: LCC PQ6662.O77 R4513 2020 (print) |
LCC PQ6662.O77 (ebook) | DDC 863/.64 — dc23
LC record available at https://lccn.loc.gov/2019024026
LC ebook record available at https://lccn.loc.gov/2019024027

Book design by Emily Snyder

Printed in the United States of America
DOC 10 9 8 7 6 5 4 3 2 1

Who lives longer than forty years? . . .
I'll tell you who: good-for-nothings and
fools.

— FYODOR DOSTOYEVSKY

I found the other people by going in the
opposite direction.

— THOMAS BERNHARD

I hate rabbits.

— EDDIE COCHRAN

I

THERE IS NO JUSTIFYING OUR OPTIMISM, NO SIGNS GIVE us reason to believe things could get better. Our optimism grows by itself, like a weed, after a kiss, a talk, a good wine, though we have very little of that left. Surrender is like that, too: the poison of defeat springs up and grows during a bad day, with the clarity of a bad day, spurred by little things that, in better circumstances, wouldn't have hurt us and yet, if the final blow happens to come right when we're at the end of our strength, manages to annihilate us. Suddenly, something that we wouldn't even have noticed before destroys us, like a trap laid by a hunter whose skill outpaces our own, a trap we didn't pay attention to because we were distracted by the lure. And yet, why deny that we ourselves, while we could, hunted in the same way, wielding traps, lures, and grotesque but highly effective camouflage.

Anyone who looks carefully at this house's garden can easily tell that it's seen better days, that the drained pool isn't out of place with the buzz of airplanes that punish us nightly, not only here on this property but throughout the valley. When she comes to bed I try to calm her, but the truth is that I know something is collapsing and we won't be able to build anything new in its place. Each bomb in this war rips open a hole we won't be able to fill, I know it and she knows it, although we pretend otherwise when it's time to go to sleep, searching for a peace we no longer find, for a time like before. On some nights, in order to dream better, we remember.

❖

In that other time, we enjoyed what we thought would be ours forever. The cool waters of the lake — we called it a lake, but it was more like a big pond — not only refreshed us on hot days, but also offered all sorts of games and safe adventures. That last thing, *safe adventures,* is without a doubt a contradiction we were unaware of at the time.

We had a small rowboat and the boys spent hours in it pretending to be pirates, and sometimes, on summer afternoons, I'd take her out on the water, as we say, and we'd each get lost in our own thoughts, not talking much, but serene.

Yesterday a letter arrived from Augusto, our son, our soldier, and it informs us that a month ago he was still alive, though that doesn't mean he isn't dead today. The joy the letter brings us also feeds our fear. Ever since the pulse signals were cut off by the provisional government's decree, we've gone back to waiting for the mail carrier, the way our grandparents did. There is no other form of communication. At least we have month-old news of Augusto, it's been almost a year since we've had word of Pablo. When they left for the front, the pulse signals still kept us constantly in touch with their heartbeats; she said it was almost like having them inside, like when she'd felt them living in her womb. Now we're forced to dream them into being, in silence. War, for parents, is not the same thing as war for the men who go and fight, it's a different war. Our only job is to wait. Meanwhile, the garden despairs and dies, worn out. She and I, on the other hand, get up every morning ready and willing.

Our love, in facing this war, is growing stronger.

It's hard to say now how much we loved each other before; obviously, the kisses at our wedding were sincere, but that sincerity is a part of what we were then, and time has clearly turned us into something else. This very morning, I walked the property to confirm yet again that this place barely resembles what our house used to be. The lake is almost dry; someone, likely the enemy, has dammed the mountain streams. The shores of the lake, once as green as the jungle, are withering.

War doesn't change anything on its own, it only reminds us, with its noise, that everything changes.

And despite the war — or thanks to the war — we carry on, good morning, good night, one day after another, just like that, one kiss after another, against all logic. The water boils, the heirloom teapot with its crocheted cozy, the last tea bags . . . the little we have left boils, is protected, goes on. Something dies and lives between us, something nameless that we decide, for good reason, to ignore. Passion either ignores misfortune or dies. We've made choices; one of them is not to be alone. To love is to defy any devil that tells us it's possible not to love.

Luckily, faced with the devil, the things that are close to us multiply.

I can talk about her hands because I know them, because they're near me. Nothing can be said about what's too far away. The boy cries in the basement, and he isn't our son but we try to care for him as best we can. We like having something to care for, on that at least we agree, despite the garden's premature death. The child arrived in the summer, more than six months ago, we don't know his age although we think he's about nine years old, we've had children and their various heights are marked in pencil on the wall of their old bedroom. We used these measurements of our own children to estimate this stranger's age, though we know it's not a precise calculation. Nor is he our son, this boy we're measuring now, but he showed up here alone and we take care of him.

He was wounded when he arrived, which was part of why we started caring for him. We're not virtuous, I know, but that makes us less merciless. Also, since our own sons left home, we've had plenty of space. We hide him in the basement because we still haven't decided what to do with him. War takes many things away and at the same time offers possibilities, which we weren't used to having, and for that reason we put off saying yes or no to the options that present themselves. People who are prepared have no fear, but we do, or at least I do — I wouldn't dare speak for her. Fear is personal, to each their own. In any case, we don't believe we've stolen a child, but prefer to believe we've taken him in.

The boy, for his part, still hasn't said a word. His silence both unsettles and consoles us, we wait for his first word and we fear it.

And what if the first thing he says isn't *thank you*?

What will we do with him then?

Sometimes he cries at night as we fuck, but we don't stop, in the old days we also managed to fuck despite the cries of our own children. We aren't crazy, that's how people conceive. It's the natural course of things. Life doesn't threaten life, but stimulates it. Yesterday I gave our prisoner a chess set; we call him that, prisoner, because we haven't given him a name, but his door has no lock. He could leave if he wanted to, just as he came here because he wanted to. Yet, he stays. I suppose the will that brought him here is the same will that keeps him here. We, in turn, feed him well from the little we have. He doesn't like bananas, that much we know, he's no monkey. Potatoes with sausage drives him wild, he's got a great temperament, he licks his fingers with gusto. It's satisfying to watch a child eat, even if he isn't your own.

He strikes us as a good kid, though we don't know where the hell he comes from. If all goes smoothly and he behaves himself, maybe we'll move him upstairs one day, to our sons' room. She insists on doing it right now, but I'm being the prudent one, his true behavior remains to be seen. It also remains to be seen whether our actual sons will survive this war and need their room back. Everything, in fact, remains to be seen, and this is my only consolation. If I've learned one thing from watching our garden die, it's that neither the good nor the bad stops to consider our plans, nor to appreciate our efforts; it simply happens.

She was the first to spot the child, she saw him walking down the hill and watched him enter our garden, bleeding but not making a sound. She brought him inside, dressed his wounds, gave him our children's small clothes that she'd kept carefully folded away, she bathed him and cooked dinner, and she made him a bed in the little playroom in the basement. I suggested that we call the police, but she said no. She preferred a child over an investigation. She knows exactly what she does and doesn't want.

That was more than six months ago, but the kid is still silent. I'd like to think he's comfortable. He's well behaved, sometimes he throws things while he's playing, though he still hasn't broken anything valuable. He doesn't look like our sons, he's dark and thin, and ours were and are, at least until their deaths are confirmed, blond and hardy. It's strange, but his presence feels more and more familiar to us. He watches television with us, we avoid sad movies, he likes comedies, he laughs. He seems happy and he eats well. The truth is, we have no complaints. She strokes his hair when he falls asleep on the sofa, and he lets her, later I carry him to bed and change his clothes. I don't dare give him a good-night kiss the way I did with our boys because, when it comes down to it, however likable this kid may be, he isn't ours.

This morning the zone agent came to inquire about our situation. It seems the war is dragging on, that bombs are falling closer to us every day, he's worried that we won't be able to hold out; naturally, we lied. Or maybe not, maybe this boy is revitalizing our capacity to hold out. The pantry is almost empty. We have little tea left and even less coffee, we drink wine in smaller glasses each day, the vegetables are gone, though we do have string beans, the sausage and chorizo and potatoes can last us another two weeks, the canned fried tomatoes another month, milk is no problem, the two cows left in the region are surviving the war miraculously if you consider the dryness of the grass; bread hasn't come since the baker was arrested, they say he wrote up secret reports and gave the enemy regular news about all of us and even hid an underground pulse unit. Impossible to know for sure, and a shame in any case, because he was a good baker. Since the war broke out, suspicions have done more damage than bullets.

The zone agent has warned us that there will be an evacuation drill next week, we don't know what we'll do with the child, not during the drill or during an actual evacuation, if there is one down the line. Before the war we never thought we'd leave this house, without saying so I think she and I both intended to die here. Now everything is different. We'll have to make other plans.

Our greatest fun is when we chase the boy after his bath; he runs, wrapped in a towel, slipping on the wood floor, but he keeps going, and she and I laugh as we run behind him holding his pajamas, she with the pants, I with the shirt. It has been a long time since we've been happy. I think she likes to watch me run like a madman, just as I like to see her smiling again. When he's finally dressed, with his pajamas on, we turn on the television and pull up the wool blanket; the coal is gone and, despite the fireplace, it's cold. We huddle together, the three of us, and watch comedies, we all like comedies. While he laughs, we put his socks on his feet. All there is left on television now is comedies and dramas, and sad songs or military marches; news and all the rest of it were taken away when the pulse network stopped, when WRIST communications were permanently cut off. Before that, by looking at your inner wrist you could know, if you wanted, all about what was happening in the world, and, more importantly, you could see and hear your loved ones in real time and follow the rhythm of their heartbeats, but the blue light that used to cover the skin of our wrists has been turned off for some time. Now we have no choice but to laugh along with comedies on television, even though we've already seen them a million times. It's something. At least the kid is amused.

When the boy has fallen asleep, she and I go to bed, exhausted, arms around each other, ready to surrender to sleep, just like before. We aren't doing anything wrong, the child arrived alone, nobody brought him, and we like to think he doesn't belong to anyone.

She and I, on the other hand, are very different. She is a lady, and before I married her I was her employee. Her life is not my life. The many things under this single roof keep their own names.

She is and always was a lady, and I, before becoming a gentleman, was a servant, everybody knows it, there's no point in hiding anything.

I was born a day laborer, but I worked my way up to foreman, and later on she educated me, against my own nature, to be a gentleman, father, and husband. She did it slowly, sweetly, and firmly, the way she does everything.

❖

The zone agent doesn't suspect anything, we have two sons fighting in this war, he treats us respectfully but his enormous responsibility and small amount of power drive him to ask too many questions. She knows how to answer him. She says no to him as if there were nothing behind it, eliminates the second question with her first response, she has a gift. During the zone agent's visit, the boy slept, or he pretended to sleep, she convinced him to and he didn't protest. The boy knows exactly what he's doing, wherever he comes from he doesn't seem wild about going back. The little warmth and food we have appear to be enough for him, and this, why deny it, reassures us. Children of your own are always more demanding. Or that's how it seemed to me. I saw so much of their mother in them that my pride mixed with responsibility and I felt I could never give them enough. Our sons, Augusto and Pablo, are less than two years apart in age, they grew up very close and enlisted together, and together they went off to war. For a man who's never fought, it's strange to have sons who are soldiers. I feel that I should be the one protecting them with my weapons, rather than the other way around. I feel useless. Our boy prisoner, who of course is no prisoner, helps me forget those thoughts and most others, too; when he smiles, I remember taking care of my own children. Sometimes, at night, I take one of my old Remington shotguns and patrol the house, I know it's ridiculous but it comforts me. Maybe I'll teach the new boy to hunt. There must be at least one fox left in the forest, I can't see it but I know it's there because I've found tooth marks in the wooden fence.

We've been given very precise instructions for the evacuation drill. What to take, in which line to stand, the identification papers we should bring. We're worried about the boy, how to hide him, what documents we can use for him. Yesterday we argued about it. She thinks that if the evacuation occurs with the enemy at our door, so to speak, there won't be time to be meticulous and no one will ask many questions, but I doubt this, I know the people in this region and the way some of them envy us, and I don't want to give them the chance to harm us. On another point we agree completely: under no circumstances can we leave the boy alone, at the mercy of the enemy or, worse, starvation if the enemy takes too long to arrive.

❖

The evacuation drill has been canceled; it seems we're out of time. Our permanent relocation was announced this morning because the war is being lost, and for our own good, as they put it to us, we should leave our homes. They will protect us better than we can protect ourselves.

It's all for our own good.

Right here, among our own, according to rumors, spies multiply and rats hide, or rats multiply and spies hide, I haven't understood it very well. What's happening is that our properties will be confiscated but respected, and maybe, in the best of all maybes, we might return one day to our own land, when the war is over and we can all trust each other again.

❖

They say the new place is cleaner than this one, an enclosed translucent space where nothing bad can hide, or hurt us. They call it the transparent city.

Those responsible for our well-being think for us while they think of us. The zone agent speaks sensibly and says what the government tells him to say. One can assume that the government knows what it's talking about, and knows why it does what it does.

We have a week to prepare for our departure. They gathered us in the town hall and explained to us that this transparent city is not an exile, not a prison, but a refuge. I don't know whether everyone understood, there was a lot of murmuring, and questions, as well as rationalizations, and more than one protest. The fish farmer asked how much time we might expect to spend in this refuge, and whether being there makes us refugees, and the zone agent explained that this is no temporary refuge, but a secure city where we can start looking toward the future. Then a woman who I think is an accountant for the local government asked whether it's true that we won't ever return, and a man in the back, whom I didn't recognize, said no way, no one could make him move, and the agent became impatient at all the questions and tried to put an end to things by saying that all relevant information would be provided on our arrival. That was enough for me, but not for my neighbors, many of whom shouted more questions and more protests, until the zone agent took out his gun and fired into the air to make everyone shut up. Silence fell over the room. He concluded by saying that our questions were beyond his ability to answer, but each of our admittedly reasonable concerns would be resolved by a higher authority when the time came.

The two of us didn't say a peep. We have our own problems.

We don't know how to hide the boy who isn't ours, we're trying to come up with a story that justifies his presence and sounds believable. When the roar of bombs dies down, suspicions grow into rumors. Every day another neighbor is arrested. No explanations are given, the guilty know perfectly well what they were up to, while the innocent are safe. Only those free of blame will go to the transparent city. Snitches are ratting out their fellow snitches. Yesterday the postmaster was taken, they say he read and resealed letters before delivering them. They say the enemy never sleeps, and could be anywhere, be anyone. We have two sons fighting in the war, and this gives us peace for now, as our sons' bravery ensures our safety and earns us respect from our neighbors. We are the parents of soldiers, and for this reason the town doesn't doubt our loyalty; nobody would betray their own children. Our problem is the boy, and we know it. We hid a boy without knowing where he came from, and that could make us appear guilty. Something must be done about the kid. As we pack our suitcases, we also plan. We speak to each other quietly at night, with the lights out, as if someone were spying on us. I think we're both afraid.

She has agreed to passing him off as our nephew, it seems the most sensible plan. Many people have died in this war, and it's not unusual for us to care for the children of our dead. I don't have any siblings, but she has two in the capital, and though they aren't the right age to be soldiers, they could have been bomb victims. You don't have to be a particular age, or fit a certain profile, to be killed by a bomb. Anyone will do. She hasn't heard from her siblings for some time now, they could be dead. The telephones stopped working more than a year ago, the mail takes a long time (and arrives already opened, it seems), so in theory anything is possible. Obviously, we're trying to think of a name for the boy, something he'll answer to or at least turn his head for. If you turn at the sound of a name, it's yours.

We can't seem to agree on a name, but we do agree that the sooner he learns it, the better, the poor kid has to get used to it. I like Julio, but she prefers Edmundo, which to me sounds long and complicated, like a fake name. If I keep insisting, I think Julio will win out. She chose our real sons' names, so it only seems fair that I get to pick the name for this stranger.

The week of our departure has arrived. At night we look at the house from the outside, from the dead garden, to start getting used to being gone. We've fucked a cou-

ple of times since they told us we'd have to leave, we don't
know whether we'll be able to keep fucking in the transparent city.

Everybody knows that transparency affects intimacy.

❖

A rumor reached us this morning, and in the afternoon
the zone agent confirmed it: we can only take a very few
things to the city. No furniture, as there will be no trucks,
and no books either, since they have books there. Two
photographs are allowed: one of your parents and one of
your children, for those who have children, but only one
photo of each child per couple, no more. In the transparent city, almost everything has to start over. No cleaning
supplies, because the provisional government is in charge
of cleaning, and nothing that stains, so as not to make
their work harder, one sports-related item, a ball, a tennis
racket, a chess set, though many people mock the idea of
chess as a sport, no weapons, because the city will protect
us, no skis, because there's no snow. One swimsuit per person, because there's a pool, eyeglasses and contact lenses
are permitted, but no medications, as those will be pre-
scribed there after a brief review of our ailments. The zone
agent says we'll be as happy there as we could be anywhere

else, and that—above all—we'll be safe. She doubts it, and I'm worried too, but what can we do? The government must be trusted, as provisional as it might be. The only alternatives are anarchy or death. Two things that neither of us really wants. I'm almost hopeful about this adventure that sounds so secure.

While we pack, we try out both names on the boy, Julio and Edmundo, and he doesn't turn for either of them, he must have a name, but we still don't know what it is because he won't say a word . . .

She shouts *Edmundo* and I shout *Julio,* but the kid pays us no mind, in the end she's worn down and gives in. He's Julio from this moment on.

❖

We're leaving very soon, they've told us that we have to burn down the house so it can't harbor any enemies, but the land will remain in our name, and after the war, the government will send official help for reconstruction if it sees fit to do so. Someone asked whether that means we'll be able to return, and the zone agent replied that it didn't mean anything, not yet, and another guy asked whether our WRISTs would be returned, and the pulse units, and the agent stated flatly that the WRIST system will never

return, as it's been proven to cause sedition, and in response to the next question — whether we'd be washing
clothes by hand or with machines — the good man got fed
up, not without reason, and began replying to everything
the same way, saying that the question is beyond what he
knows or can do.

It's clear that the zone agent doesn't have much more
information than the rest of us about what's going on or
where we're headed. I have to admit that I figured this out
a long time ago, which is why I don't ask any questions. I
won't take any delicate clothing, to be safe. Who knows if
everything will get washed together, or what.

They've given us two cans of gasoline to burn down
our home. Of course I've thought about using them to fill
the tank of our car and driving off on our own, but the
cars were seized yesterday, because they'd thought of the
same thing. We'll be going to the transparent city in air-
conditioned buses. The train tracks have been sabotaged.

Burning down our house won't be easy. She cries just
thinking about it, and I try to console her, not because I'm
not sad too, but because over the years I've become the one
who provides comfort. Also, the house is hers, and before
that it belonged to her first husband's family, so it's under-
standable that this would really crush her soul.

She, like all women, is stronger than any man, but
sometimes she breaks and I hug her. I do it without think-

ing, it's what I've done all my life. My father did the same
with my mother.

Julio smiles like none of this has anything to do with
him, his innocence protects him, at least for now; if one
day they discover that he isn't ours, he'll learn . . . well,
may God keep him from it.

We only have two days left to burn everything and get
out of here, the suitcases are packed. We've slept terribly,
but that's something anyone in their right mind could understand, you don't abandon the place that's been your
home just like that, plus the moon has been full. Last
night, the white light slid between the curtains and we had
no choice but to stare at what was until very recently ours,
and to see it all with unbearable clarity.

At dawn we finally surrendered to sleep.

WE WOKE TO JULIO'S CRIES. SOMETIMES WHEN HE'S having nightmares, Julio weeps like a baby. We don't know what he dreams, because he still won't say a word, but he calms down when he's in her arms. Children and animals have a hard time adjusting to change, and he senses that we're leaving, he's seen his suitcase, he's also seen the cans of gasoline in the living room, though I can't tell whether he knows what we must do with them.

He's had a good breakfast, we've given him almost everything we had left although she's hidden a few cans among our clothes, though we've been assured that there will be food. She's not quick to trust, and I don't blame her. After washing up, we took a walk around the property, all the way to the forest. We don't know when we'll be able to return, which made the walk strange. Not for Julio, he was happy, climbing trees, chasing flies; squirrels have been gone for some time. It's hard to know what a child is thinking, but it's clear that daytime doesn't scare him, only his dreams do. We are scared of the days, of real things, of knowing that we may never return, of not knowing who we'll be when we come back if that day ever arrives. Of course I took my shotgun to the forest, and I even shot at a sparrow. I don't usually shoot birds, but there isn't anything else left in the forest now. I don't know when I'll be able to hunt again, weapons are forbidden in the transparent city. In any case, I have no intention of burning my shotguns along with my house, I've decided to bury them in pillowcases when she and the boy are asleep. I won't tell them about it—not them, not the zone agent, not anyone. A man does what he likes with his shotguns. As it should be.

Julio has gotten lost in the forest a couple of times, we've called to him with his new name and he's returned. At least I've hit the mark on one thing. Julio is a good name.

We've gathered berries and a few flowers, we want our last dinner to be special. Anything that doesn't happen often is special, and the most special things are those that might never happen again.

I don't know whether I've mentioned this, but she's a formidable cook. The old potatoes have a bitter edge, and her sweet tomato sauce blunts it. She has many other talents beyond the kitchen, she often helps me not to cry, and at other times she entertains me with her over-the-top stories. That's something I admire in her that I never learned: how to make up stories. It's no wonder that Julio is almost always by her side now that he knows his name, and even before he knew it. Our children did the same thing. People who know how to tell stories always have company.

❖

After a lot of folding and pressing, hiding and removing, choosing and tossing, we packed our three suitcases with the essentials for our life in the transparent city. We've left them next to the front door.

This is the house where our children were born, and where they had their first sip of milk from a wet nurse who died before the war but because of this war. She was a foreigner, from the enemy's land, and she was displaced as tension was rising, soon after the murder of the Twelve Righteous Ones. The Twelve Righteous Ones were murdered for their faith, which is strange when you consider that nobody around here ever believed in much of anything at all, but the Twelve Righteous Ones prayed and were the first to fall. A single bomb took them all out, and though the guilty party was never found, the enemy was immediately blamed for the tragedy. The newspapers declared that war was imminent, and deportations began. Our wet nurse died in a refugee camp near the border. Our children had forgotten her by the time they left for war, and we never told them about her. When the war broke out, Augusto was nine and Pablo was eight. They've spent most of their lives in wartime, but we did what we could to shield them. It's only been three years since bombs became audible nearby, before that it was easy to make them believe that this war didn't exist. For a long time, we lived far from the misfortune. This was before misfortune spread across mountain and valley, town and forest, and all over the land, before fear invaded our whole region, before news arrived that the capital had fallen, before all that.

❖

She and I understood that our sons would be soldiers if the war dragged on, which is why we secretly followed the news and hoped for a truce that never came. The war has lasted more than a decade, the longest one we've seen in our lives. The wet nurse had a sweet face, weathered in the way of someone who's worked outdoors from sunup to sundown since childhood, and her breasts were pale and generous. We never believed she could harm us, but the government thought differently. It's easier for a man to be trusting, but a government has to be careful, protect its long-term interests. Those with the most responsibility must be the most vigilant. That's how it should be, I think, and that's why I put up no resistance when they took the wet nurse, and that's why my wife didn't say anything in her defense either, though the wet nurse had so tenderly cared for our boys and had never, to our knowledge, wished us harm.

Little by little they took all the domestic workers, the immigrants who cared for the garden and the land, and then the boys lined up and left, and in the end we were alone until the arrival of this kid, Julio, whom we don't want to lose. I look out at the land and don't see any of what we cultivated with our own hands. No harvested grain, no baskets of fruit, no wood to chop, no weeds to pull among the rose bushes, all of it overrun with the same weeds now, formless, not a flower in sight. Nor do any weasels or dormice poke their heads between the plants, no vermin hide among the roof tiles, no wasps bang against the windows. There aren't even any robbers to ward off with my gun, nor any foreigners left to hang. Nobody comes through here anymore except the zone agent, and his mere presence seems to keep away all beasts, large and small. All that's left of what was ours is the shadow of our house, and the house itself. The names of those who've slept under our roof and in the stables are slipping from memory, and we can't remember anyone but Augusto and Pablo, our two soldiers. We used to get letters from Augusto occasionally, but never from Pablo. Any day now they'll kill our boys, if they haven't already. That's what she's always saying: any day now they'll kill our boys. She says it constantly, and I tell her no, woman, no, but she repeats it as if she hasn't heard me. Once she puts her mind to something, no one can stop her, she's as stubborn as a mule. If she wants to make cakes, she does it, even if there isn't any sugar, and then she gets angry if I don't eat them. But she's a good woman, capable and clean, and though she was raised as a lady, she can do backbreaking work like a champ. When our mares were taken, she turned the lever at the well with her bare hands. They blistered, but she didn't stop until we had enough water to get through the day. Running water was cut off at the beginning of the war, maybe before that, when war was no more than a word spoken over and over as if it were the only word left.

The first zone agent told us the water was going to stop running, so we filled the bathtubs and all our pitchers like they would last forever, then lived off rainwater caught by the well and prayed there would be no more droughts, and

when drought came anyway, we bought water from the
tanker trucks with her four remaining pieces of antique
jewelry. We have no jewelry left now, nor barely anything
that could be used to barter with, and the little we do have
covers only potatoes and milk. The earth is becoming barren as no one is farming it, and soon there won't be anything left to eat in the valley, which is why it's not so bad
that they'll be taking us away from here and burning down
our house, or making us burn it down. It's almost certain
we'll be better off in the government's care than on our
own, since taking care of ourselves in this barren land isn't
possible anymore. A man who doesn't provide for his family shrinks and shrinks until he no longer exists, and before that happens he must accept in good faith what the
government offers. In the new city, they'll tell us how we
can earn a living, and it seems from what the zone agent
says that tasks and jobs have been planned for everyone
in accordance with our abilities, so that no one freeloads
or gets restless for lack of things to do, because laziness is
bound to lead to problems. When we arrive we'll be given
employment, nothing important at first, but enough for us
to have a place and not disturb the overall flow of things,
the normal, the necessary, since in that city, according to
what's being said, noise and disturbances are strictly forbidden, which I must admit puts my mind at ease, because all
good things require an atmosphere of order, and the rest is
a breeding ground for good-for-nothings, bums, and petty

thieves, who, the second you let your guard down, multiply among citizens who wear decency on their sleeves. If one thing has been made clear about what we're to find in the new city, it's that no excess or ruckus will be allowed, that there will be people who monitor us to make sure everything is as it should be, since, with many people living in close quarters, the crooked shatter under pressure, and these shattered pieces become splinters or kindling for a larger fire. Back when people worked the land, each person took care of his business and there was room for everyone, but if we have to live together, cramped and unarmed, it's better that we be monitored and not have to pay for what others get up to. She says she can't imagine what life will be like there, and I tell her it doesn't matter, there's no point trying to imagine what will soon come to pass. We've told the boy Julio about the move, and he either doesn't care or doesn't understand, because he's kept on smiling as if none of this has anything to do with him. He hasn't been in our home long enough to be attached to it, and he never saw our land when it was rich and beautiful, so that's not a loss to him. He never played with the horses or hunted in the forest, and the fact is he's barely seen the best of what this house or the two of us have to offer. He'll have nothing to compare to the future, nor will whatever's coming bear the shadow of our past. He won't lose any friends in the move, since there are no children left on any of the nearby farms or even in town, the last of them were taken by hunger or the flu; the older kids are off at war, and the only adult males left are the old men from town, the gypsies of the valley, and, on the hill beyond the forest, the water owners, husband and wife, who sell us water from tanker trucks during droughts, but the water owners are very important people, the kind you see only during public holidays, and even then you barely say a word to them out of respect, or perhaps out of fear, which everyone has for them. In all this time I've barely exchanged more than a good morning or good afternoon with the water owners. She, on the other hand, has something of a friendship with the water owner's wife, also referred to as the water owner, because the water was actually hers first, inherited from her father. She used to have my wife over for tea in her mansion once in a while, but her husband didn't want her to be so friendly with the neighbors, and after that my wife never set foot in the water owners' luxurious rooms again. Our house is very nice, I'm not complaining or anything, but theirs is a mansion as God intended, with so many servants that, when they gather for a hunt, they look like an army. She's asked me whether the water owners' mansion will also be burned down, and I've told her I don't think so, because such important people would surely be treated differently, despite the war and the evacuation; plus, I've heard the postmen in town gossiping that the water owners might not be relocated at all, and that if they are, they won't go with the regular group but with another one headed to a different place, a better one I suppose, given their importance. All kinds of things are said in town and no one knows what's really true, and people always say strange things about the rich, mostly out of envy. It doesn't make sense to go around making predictions, because soon enough we'll all find out what's what, when we get in line to leave we'll see who's coming with us and who isn't.

I'm in charge of burning the house because I don't want her to hurt herself, not for anything in the world. I'll do it the way they told us to and use the gasoline cans we were given. I don't understand why so much gasoline is being wasted in times like these, when you think about it I could burn the house with just a bit of alcohol and cardboard and wool, but the orders arrive on officially embossed paper and it's always best to obey these types of papers without complaints or questions, since not doing so could raise suspicions, especially when there's a war going on and enemies will take advantage of anything that could harm morale.

This caring for her so much isn't new, because I've always taken care of her as best I could, when I was foreman of this land, and later when she was widowed, and when, soon after that, she became mine. Horrible things were said in town about our love, but it's not true that I dared look her in the eyes, nor that I defied her husband while he was still alive; it was her love that gave me this land, not my ambition. She chose me to carry the name of this house, she gave me books to read, she taught me with great patience, until I was no longer the man I'd been and transformed into the one I am today. She never told our children anything about the past, never told them that before I oversaw the laborers, I was a laborer myself. They found this out at school, and if it hurt them we never learned of it, as we raised them to be strong, quiet, and solid, which is why they're such good soldiers, the three medals on one of their chests and two medals on the other prove it. Medals for courage, not for favors or office work, real medals for real soldiers. When we think they might be dead, which we do every so often, turning our imagination to the medals doesn't ease our pain or our fear, but I do notice how they pull at the hems of our pride, at the threads of that regal garment every parent wears when looking at their children from a distance, though of course we'd rather have them by our side again, safe and sound.

When I burn the house, I don't want her to see it, not even a bit, which is why I told her to wait at the bus stop, which is where we've been told the women will gather while the men destroy everything to protect it all from the enemy. That's what was written on the official notice the zone agent gave us, and that's what we'll do, because when it comes to government matters, there should be no nonsense or delay. Each person's pain is their own business, and there's no use going around crying like children when what's required of us is action, courage, and strategy. The zone agent has taken the time to explain everything

so as to avoid errors or confusion, and he's mentioned in
a low voice, like a man going beyond the call of duty out
of friendship and trust, that for the government's plan to
succeed, the obedience and goodwill of each participant
will be of utmost importance. Though we'll be forming a
line, we are not kids, and the final victory depends in great
measure on our own effort and tenacity. That's how he put
it to us, and if it sounded like propaganda it wasn't his fault,
but rather the fault of those who taught him to say what
he says. Before this zone agent, we had another one who
spoke in the same way, but that one was killed because of
suspicions, so really, being a zone agent who repeats all the
government's instructions to the letter guarantees nothing; here, the minute a rumor sticks to you, you're fucked.
She's the one who taught me to question what they tell us,
because before I was a man of labor rather than of letters,
and she's also the one who taught me to obey despite my
doubts, that one thing doesn't impede the other. The way
she explained it to me, or the way I've understood it, is that
you obey because it's to your advantage to do so, and you
doubt because you think. And if one of those things saves
your life, the other seems to save your soul. That's how
she's persuaded me to carry forward our little ploy and not
tell anyone about our Julio, not what we know and not
what we can imagine, and instead to breathe life into the
lie we've come up with, which she refers to as our story.

   She says that it's the story that matters and not the reality that binds it. Since she's much more intelligent than I am, I listen to her about everything, and when it comes to her, I neither doubt nor obey but act out of free will and conviction. Abandoning the boy to his own fate doesn't seem like a godly thing to do, and we know that caring for defenseless children, whether they have a name or not, is just and good in the eyes of the Lord, and cannot bring anything bad to our hearts.

She left for town at dusk, suitcase in hand, it's almost a two-hour walk but she's strong and her pace is so brisk it takes effort to keep up with her. She's left the boy with me because I asked her to, I think the house will make a spectacular fire once night falls, and there is no child who doesn't love to watch a fire.

The kid has helped me with the gasoline cans, and we've splashed every room and then, more carefully, the foundation. I didn't let him use the lighter, because it's not like I want him to turn into a pyromaniac or have too much fun with something that, at the end of the day, as important as it might be to the provisional government, signifies the end of everything we were and had.

As I watched the house burn, surprise rushed in where I thought I'd feel sorrow. It burned so quickly that it seemed to be made of toothpicks instead of sturdy wood, and soon, as the boy and I rubbed the heat and sparks from our eyes, it didn't exist at all.

I suppose that's how everything disappears.

THERE WAS A TREMENDOUS UPROAR AT THE BUS STOP, and when the kid and I arrived, lost in a crowd of so many sad faces and all of them the same and so very many people, it took us a good while to find her. How happy it made us to be together again! Like we hadn't seen each other in a long time, though it'd been only a few hours. Night was well under way and the buses still hadn't arrived, but according to the zone agent, the first and foremost thing to do was form orderly rows, collect names,

and examine suitcases. At first count, thirty extra people
had appeared, but they were all gypsies and were immediately removed — not without a racket, of course, these being gypsies, the second you do anything to them they weep
and shout like they're being flayed. It had been made very
clear, both in writing and aloud, that gypsies would not be
going to the transparent city with the rest of us, so who
knows why they made such a scene. In any case, they were
removed from the line and despite the big fuss they had no
choice but to return to the valley. I've never had a problem with gypsies, no good feelings and no bad; if I saw them
near the stables, the chickens, or the orchards, I'd take up
my shotgun and that would be that. There's no gypsy in
the world who doesn't respect a shotgun. Once they were
gone, another count took place, and that second winnow-
ing yielded only two who didn't belong, not gypsies but
foreigners. They were taken aside and carefully stripped of
their suitcases, without a word as to what would happen
to them, though I'd guess they would go right to a prison
camp. It seemed that nobody knew them, and anyone who
did know them pretended not to. I had no need to lie, as
I'd never seen them before in my life. They were a young
couple, clearly deserters, at least he was, considering that if
he'd been from here and as healthy as he looked, at his age
he'd be a soldier at war, just like our sons. Nobody has said
anything about Julio, it's obviously assumed that he's family; we're from here, and we have some status, with two

sons who are, if not heroes, at least soldiers. I pray for everything to go well, and swallow hard.

They haven't removed anyone else from the line, though they have confiscated a lot of items from people, because, though the government paper stated each person could bring only one small suitcase, there are some who seem to have brought everything with them except the wall clock and the marriage bed. I even saw a cello confiscated—you've got to be off your rocker to try to bring a cello on a bus for refugees. As if we'd try to form a band.

When our turn arrived, we showed our papers, but the zone agent knew us well, and there were no problems except for the boy, which we'd expected. I let her do the talking, since she's a lady to the marrow of her bones and could explain it all without a tremble in her voice, and she spoke from such great heights that the agent lowered his gaze and even stroked our false nephew's hair affectionately and with great pity when she said he'd been recently orphaned and was shaken, almost mute with pain. The kid behaved splendidly and put on such a sad face that, had he been a film actor, he'd have won an award. Meanwhile, my hands were clammy with sweat up until the moment the zone agent stamped our papers with the official seal and moved on to the next people in line. While he was talking to us and asking about the kid, I did hear people murmuring, but it's not like they knew enough about us to understand our affairs, we only came down the hill and into town for holidays, for any major shopping I'd drive to the city in our car. I've always known that we were envied, and it should come as no surprise, because aside from the water owners we had the biggest house in the region. As it happened, just as I told her, the water owners weren't at the bus stop, and though I didn't say anything, it stupidly made me happy that I'd been right. Just as well, because if I'd said something, I would have ended up looking like a complete idiot. When everyone in line had been registered, the water owners arrived in a car, with a chauffeur and everything. The car wasn't theirs, it belonged to the government, and had an official license plate and a national flag attached to the antenna. I was so surprised to see them that I pulled on her sleeve, as the agent had requested, or rather demanded, silence. She calmed me by pressing my hand, as if to convey that nothing could surprise her anymore.

The water owners didn't get out of the car until everything was ready, nor did they present their papers to the zone agent, and when three buses finally arrived, they got on the first one, cutting to the front of the line we stood in, while the rest of us waited patiently. Once they were inside, the rest of us were told to board one at a time, in the order in which we stood. When she and I boarded, I don't know why, but it calmed me to see the owners there, and without greeting anyone we settled in as quickly as possible in the back, almost in the last row. The zone agent inspected the three buses one by one, and counted us all one more time. He also congratulated us on fulfilling the procedures with discipline, and encouraged us to relax a bit and chat if we liked, as the trip would be a long one.

We placed the boy between us, so that the three of us occupied only two seats. We put our suitcases in the compartment over our heads, they were small suitcases, as had been requested. She kissed the boy on the forehead as the bus started to move, then she kissed me on the lips. We now had permission to talk, but I couldn't think of anything to say.

We took the road toward the city, and as we passed the hill I saw smoke rising from our house, but on the other side of the forest I saw no smoke at all. The water owners' mansion had not been burned, so I'd at least been right about that. Soon after we left the valley, we detoured off the main highway onto the region's old road, passing the harbor, leaving the lake behind us, then crossing into the neighboring region. As we passed through the next town over, we saw that it was empty, it must have been evacuated first, and as we drove on we saw one deserted village after another, and I could tell they'd been depopulated recently because there were still objects on the streets, clothes, furniture, open suitcases, and even lights left on in a window here and there, perhaps more out of forgetfulness than because anyone was still inside, and in this manner towns passed by us like ghosts without names until we were so far from home that I didn't recognize a thing. The child was sleeping, and the chatter on the bus had died down until almost nobody was talking anymore and only snores filled the bus. She was awake, staring out of the window, it was hard to tell what she was thinking, and when I asked, she said that she wasn't thinking about anything, except perhaps about what the transparent city would be like and whether it would be made of glass or crystal or some other see-through material, and whether we'd have enough room to be comfortable, and whether there would be a school or other children at least, though the part about a school didn't bother her too much, as she herself could certainly teach Julio what he needed to learn. She wasn't wrong about that, before she took me as her lover and then her husband, I barely knew my arithmetic, or how to handle invoices or records, and about the greater world I knew nothing, nothing at all, that is to say, I knew how to work with my hands, and how to read and write in a pinch, but not much more. I could do things but not think about them, and it was she, with her books, who taught me little by little how to imagine and remember, how to clearly express my ideas and emotions. With her help, I learned quickly, though I would never call myself bright. With our sons, who came from her and had her blood, and therefore her superior intelligence, she'd done an even better job, and they talked in a way that made you love to just listen. To me, a man who's never met anyone of importance, they sounded like princes. Our new kid, Ju-

lio, seems pretty smart, though he hasn't spoken yet, so I
have no doubt that she'll know how to turn him into an
able, educated young man. Of course, if he keeps being
mute, he'll run into problems. But all things considered,
with the war, maybe not as many problems as those who
talk too much.

Since she seemed tired, I stopped asking her questions and closed my eyes for I don't know how long, and
I dreamed that I was hunting with my real sons and that
we were killing a wild boar and a rabbit, and that's where I
was, inside my dream, skinning those animals, when I was
woken by the sound of planes. At first, planes buzz, and
then immediately the bombs shriek down, and over time
you get used to waking up fast, the way people do when
children cry in the middle of the night. After the bombs
shriek, you quickly say whatever prayers you know, just
as you might when you see lightning and fear the thunder
that might follow. Three bombs fell. The first two didn't
hit anything, they only left two huge holes one hundred
meters from the highway; the last bomb hit the middle
bus. Our driver stopped, but the water owner, the husband, stood up and ordered him to go on, and the driver
obeyed. I don't know whether the water owner is still in
charge of anything in here, but some people have given so
many orders that their voices inspire obedience. The zone
agent isn't with us, and I don't know whether he's in the
second bus, the one the bomb destroyed, or in the third

bus, I don't even know whether he's traveling with us or he stayed in town.

In any case, we've kept on, and the planes have left, and we don't know what happened to the bus that was hit, though most likely all the people in it are dead. She's clasped me so tightly that I'm sure I'll have bruises, but the boy Julio didn't even wake up, and we've laughed about that, about how this poor kid can sleep through bombs, although I also think we were laughing out of happiness that the three of us are still alive, that we got on this bus and not the other one. We didn't look back for a good long while, to avoid seeing the dead, or worse, a wounded person left to his horrible fate.

When we finally do turn to look, there's nothing left to see, and the two remaining buses drive on through the night toward wherever it is we're going. The driver has turned off his headlights, in case the planes return, and he's going more slowly, even though there's a nice big moon and you can see what's ahead. And we're probably visible, too. Soon enough, we spy the first light of day, and the headlights become useless anyway, nor is there any false darkness under which to hide. The trip is so long that I start thinking we must be near the border, but since we haven't had any reliable news about the war for months now, it's hard to know whether the border is in the same place and how much territory still belongs to us versus the enemy. During wars, maps are often good for only a few

days, with all the movement of troops here and there, forward and in retreat; the lines are stripped away and only
soldiers' feet mark what's this or that, yours or mine. With
the little I've seen of this country, and with what a poor
student of geography I was, it's hard for me to establish
where we are exactly, but it seems strange that the transparent city, or the glass or crystal city, or the whatever-
it's-made-of city, could be so close to what until very recently was enemy land. It's also possible that, despite this
evacuation and all the shortages, we're winning this war,
that we're conquering more of them than they are of us.
On the bus, breakfast has begun, since everyone brought
something for the first day at least, not bread, as there
hasn't been any of that since the baker was found guilty
of snitching, but something, a bit of cured meat or dried
herring. We're fine on water, because the water owner
brought a nice big six-liter container, which I suppose is
why his orders still carry weight and are followed to the
letter. He is, without a doubt, the highest in command on
this bus, since he's the one who distributes the water, and
because he gave the driver the first drink, you might say
he's got him in his pocket, and well paid. As the second in
command — a role he takes up once he's slaked his thirst
— the driver has instructed us over the loudspeaker not to
drink more than the cup we're given, that the journey is
long and there's still quite a way to go before reaching our
destination. So that's what we've done. It's not the water

owner, of course, who's hauled the water container down the aisle between the seats, but rather the man who'd been sitting just behind him, who, thanks to that coincidence, has found himself charged with an important responsibility and has carried it out with all the rigor of a general keeping his troops in order. If someone asked for more water, the good man would immediately raise his hand as if to deliver a blow, and nobody will argue with that. After the little rations of water were distributed, the people exchanged their good mornings and other chatter, but with so many people talking at once, it's been impossible to understand a thing, and the clamor on the bus was not so different from the clamor in town, the noise people make when they're together. Julio has woken up very hungry, and we've given him a can of tuna and our last strip of bacon. He's thanked us with kisses. He'd kissed her before, but it's the first time he's kissed me. I felt a lot of love for him then, and the urge to take care of him.

We've arrived at midday without planes or any more attacks, but through the windows we see scorched earth that looks like the end of the whole world, and there are so many bomb craters and graves marked with rifles stuck into the earth that we could swear nobody but us is left alive. The landscape resembles the places we know, but it's another place. I haven't traveled much, but I imagine that the entire earth is like this from one end to the next — that is to say, the same. From the books she gave me to read while trying to teach me, I concluded that things aren't too different around the world and that's why people dress in different colors and sing different songs, to dream for a while that they're different in some way.

We'd been getting hungry and thirsty ever since the water container had been put away, stashed safely at its owner's feet, when a tire burst with a gunshot sound. At first I thought it was another attack, but immediately the bus began to swerve on its deflated wheel and the driver shouted, *it's a flat!* And when the water owner asked for clarification, the driver, slowing to a stop, informed us of what was going on over the loudspeaker, leaving no room for doubt. Ladies and gentlemen, he said very calmly into his microphone, we have a flat, and since I have no spare tire, the journey will continue from here on foot.

The water owner, the de facto commander in charge of our trip, asked for further explanation and suggested switching the placement of the tires, but the driver replied that, in case nobody had noticed, this was not an eighteen-wheeler, nor a vehicle that ran on ten tires, or eight, but rather a small, old bus with four wheels and no spare tires, and that without another tire there was nothing to be done, and a human being was better off on his own two feet than inside an old bus that had only three wheels. Once these explanations had satisfied, which took more than a little effort, the water owner told us to exit in an orderly manner and wait for the last bus to arrive and offer

help. The driver told him that the third bus—which was
the second bus now that a bomb had fallen on the middle one—had already passed us. At this, the water owner's
authority was undermined, or at least diminished. He still
had what was left in the water container, which was, given
the circumstances, everybody's water, and nobody dared
challenge his power, though there was increased mutter-
ing from dissidents, who exist in any group. Whether or
not we had faith, we all got off the bus—why stay inside it if it doesn't work anymore? We disembarked in the
same order in which we'd gotten on, first her, the one who
takes care of us, then the boy, who matters so much to us,
and finally me, the man who's here in case anything goes
wrong. Once our feet hit the ground, new groups formed,
and new plans, with some wanting to return, others wanting to keep going and find the transparent city themselves
without knowing where it was, while others among us sat
down to wait for orders without knowing who would give
them. The water owner backed the driver, thinking, and
I believe he was right to think, that if he'd known how to
get us there by bus, he'd also know the way by foot. The
most important thing, of course, was to find out how far
we were from our new home, as we had enough water for
a day if we drank less than camels, and after that, unless
anyone knew the exact locations of wells or lakes or rivers
along the way, we'd inevitably start dying. This sparked the
first major conflict, because, according to the driver, the

city was at least two days away on foot, and that was at the pace of the strongest, and there was only enough water for one day of everyone walking together, or for both days for only the fastest among us.

It was no easy task to divide us in two, because at the end of the day we all in principle have the same rights, so there was no choice but to resort to force. When no other strategy works, force prevails, so we formed groups of the strong, and I had no trouble heading mine, as I've worked the land so much, since before I even learned to read, that my arms are as thick as clubs. While we argued over all these issues, she didn't say a word, nor did she leave my side, and she kept the boy tucked beneath her skirt, knowing that only death could tear them away from me. As always happens when two groups are formed, we, beside the stalled bus, we immediately split again — into four. Among the men, there were some who were stronger than me, but they were less rugged, and nobler, and they were trying to protect more people than they reasonably could. I was only looking after two, whom I would defend with my life if I had to, and as soon as anyone tried to push me, I'd let it be known that this wouldn't be my first fight and that, when sober and determined, I was almost impossible to knock down. The four groups formed almost naturally, each vying to travel with the water, and at the sight of us all finally divided up and silent, I think we were all gripped with fear of hurting one another, because acting like you're ready to fight is one thing, and real fighting is another. So it was left for the water owner to decide who would join him. The man who'd carried the water container on the bus immediately went to his side, because he'd grown fond of power and water, the driver had no qualms and knew it was better to accept a master than to wander this land alone. Two men from our town, who'd worked for the dam and who hauled tree trunks as if they were feathers, joined also, and we almost didn't make it into the winning group, except that the water owner was struck by the way I jostled against the weaker people with bad intentions, and, above all, because his wife fondly recalled the teas she and my wife had enjoyed together.

It was his wife who gestured to us as the final chosen ones, pointing as she whispered our names into her husband's ear.

Those two, the water owner said, and then we go.

There are three of us, my wife said.

However many it is, and we're off, the water owner's wife said, and when it came down to it the water that supplied our valley and the little that remained in the container all belonged to her, she'd inherited it from her father. Water that bore her name, and hers alone.

⬧

The water owner was not so different from me, a man who'd married above his station, the only difference being that where shame kept me silent, he got louder. He raised his voice so much that he gave the impression that everything was his, when we knew it wasn't. I neither liked nor disliked him, and I walked behind him because the driver knew where we were going and was at his side, but it's not as if I'd sworn my loyalty to him, nor did I owe him a thing. When our group was complete, there was no need for head counts, as there were only eight of us, plus Julio. The two water owners, the driver, the man who carried the water container, the two former dam workers, her, and me. My wife and the water owner's wife walked together, arm in arm, which gave the boy and me a certain status, because we were connected to them, even though we were walking toward the back, a few paces away. We'd left the suitcases on the bus. Despite our careful choosing of what to take and what to leave behind, we knew they'd be too much of a burden on the road. In any case, before we left town, the zone agent had told us that in the transparent city we'd be given everything we needed to live. I kept only the photographs of my sons; it was already hard enough to have no news of them, and I feared I would end up forgetting their faces. She, with all her foresight, took the little food we had left, as the road would be long and we'd want it when hunger mauled us. The water owners' things would be transported separately, I suppose, in trucks. Important people don't carry things, and their possessions were probably waiting for them in the city. We walked almost in single file for a long time over the plains. After passing a few hills, the land began to twist and turn, and before we could see the mountains, those of us who were country people quickly understood that the ground was sloping. Our feet grew heavy, and we had to put in twice the effort to get from one step to the next. The driver walked in front, checking his map, looking for shortcuts, because, he said, and the man had a point, following the highway is one thing when you're traveling by bus and another thing when you're on foot, when there might be shorter routes. The water owner walked behind the driver, glancing behind him now and then to see whether the women were still following him and, I'm guessing, also to see how much they were chatting. No man likes his wife to talk too much, because in women's laughter and complaints he's bound to catch a blow. I, from my place in the back, only glanced at my wife to make sure her steps were steady and she didn't need my help, I've never been afraid of what she does and doesn't say, perhaps because the worst about me was already spoken at our wedding and there's nothing left to be said. In fact, now that we're roaming free, without any land or possessions, I'm realizing that I love her more than ever and without a trace of embarrassment. Maybe it's this uphill slope that equalizes everything, but I think at this very moment and possibly for the first time I truly love her, without the shame of having been her employee before, and with more daring than I knew I had when I first became her husband.

If I'm glancing at her a lot, it's from fear that she might trip, and because, seeing her like this, from a distance, she looks all the more beautiful. I'm not one for poetry, but any man who's loved even a little bit knows what I'm talking about. To look at a woman is nothing like embracing her, because when she's in your arms, you're deeply close to each other and everything is covered up, while at a distance, without you there, the woman you love becomes something to admire from afar. That's what was on my mind—how I loved her more and better than ever, and how I had to keep the kid from falling behind chasing grasshoppers—when the man who carried the water container stepped on a mine, and in a single second we were reduced to seven. The little that remained of that man, the water container man, couldn't have been sewn back together by the best surgeon in the world. The minefields aren't from this war, but from the one before it, and some of them were still in the ground, I'd heard of people in the mountains stepping on them because they weren't paying attention. The mines are visible among the weeds, as there are marks around them; moles smell them and surround them, and the dirt over them is uneven. The water container man wasn't originally from the country,

I thought I might have seen him at the grocery store, but I'm not sure about that, and that's why he stepped on the mine. It was horrible to see, and the women closed their eyes. The water container had fallen and rolled down a cliff, and one of the dam workers had to climb down to retrieve it, and by some miracle he didn't break his neck on the rocks, but managed to return with the container and carry it until nightfall. We men drank only once, just before sunset, the boy acted like a man and drank when I did, and the women drank twice, but in little sips, because if women are ladies, they barely open their mouths when they drink or do anything else, and these two women in particular, my wife and the other one, were ladies from the cradle to the grave, as my mother used to say, and ladies like these can be spotted from far away and without even knowing their names, mostly because they barely open their mouths, and when they do it's for good reason and with purpose. As an example, I'll tell you that my wife picked up an abandoned helmet in the hills, stained with blood, and though it disgusted the rest of us, she said that once clean it would make a good soup pot, and we had no choice but to admit she was right, and later she cleaned it in a few seconds with dirt and leaves, and those who hadn't yet known saw that she was a reliable woman, which I'd known the whole time.

As twilight deepened, an argument broke out between the former dam workers. About why we couldn't stop for

the night, about whether the group knew where it was going, about why the water owner was in charge when there
was barely any water left, and they went back and forth like
this until one told his companion that if the water owner
was in charge, it wasn't because of the water but because
he had a gun with him at all times. I took all of this in as I
walked behind them, and I was glad that someone in our
group was armed, and hoped it was true. The way things
stood, we were going to sleep out in the open, and you
can sleep better outside with weapons by the fire. Without
weapons there's no order, there's nothing, and when the
water owner called for us to stop and rest, as we had finally
reached the shelter of a thicket of trees, we all obeyed like
that pistol existed, and when he proposed we make a fire
for the soup, we got right to it, though we didn't know yet
what the hell kind of soup it would be.

While the women gathered the food they'd brought, we
men looked for branches and something for the broth. Not
the water owner, though, or the driver, they sat and stud-
ied the map to see whether we were headed in the right
direction, it was the rest of us who set out for kindling. I
don't see anything wrong or unusual about those in charge
sitting down to think while the rest of us go out and do
things, because that's how I've always understood the government, and that's what I did when I went from laborer
to foreman, and then from foreman, though it was out of
love, to owner.

The larger of the two former dam laborers, a man at least my size, jokingly remarked that we could have made a nice soup from the bones of the water container man, and it goes without saying that we all looked at him with contempt and removed him, without a word, from the short list of our sympathies. When you're in a group by force and not by choice, it's hard to decide whom you like more and whom less, and you're thankful when some idiot identifies himself early on, so that everyone else can immediately feel better and know whom they wouldn't miss. In this case we couldn't possibly have made a wiser choice, because the larger dam worker, in addition to quickly tiring of the search for branches and only bringing the dampest ones, as if he had no idea how to make a fire, was drinking secretly from a flask he wasn't sharing even with his old coworker. I saw all of this, and so did Julio, as we gathered dry wood and dead leaves. And we also saw the fight that took place between them, the dam workers, when the smaller one wanted some of the larger one's wine. And we saw the way the smaller one struck the large man with a stone until he was senseless, and stole his wine, and then we watched him run off like a criminal, unaware that what he was carrying wasn't enough for the long road ahead. Julio and I approached the dead man — indeed, he was dead from the stoning — and, given that nothing could be done for him anymore, we searched his pockets for coins or anything else, and found cigarettes. And right there, a couple of paces from the dead man, the boy and I shared a smoke, and we stashed what was left, ten more cigarettes, a treasure considering the circumstances and the fact that my wife had forbidden me from smoking long before the war began, when I stopped being her employee and started being her lover. I don't see anything wrong with kids smoking when they're young, because that's how I became a man, and though now they tell me it's very bad, I'm not a doctor nor do I want to be one, and so I have no reason to pay any mind to what the medical experts say. This was not the kid's first cigarette, that much was certain, because he didn't cough or anything, and he took drags like the manliest of sailors.

When we'd smoked the cigarettes, we went back together, the kid and I, not whistling exactly, I wouldn't say that, but almost, as when it came down to it, we were free from blame. I told the remaining members of the group — the driver, the water owner, and our two wives — that the dam workers had run off and were now traveling alone at their own risk, even though this wasn't true. Nobody seemed to care that much, since the little soup there was would now spread further among us. The fewer people sit down to eat, the more you can eat, as my townspeople used to say. When she took me aside and asked me, I told her the truth, because I don't know how to lie to her. I told her that one man had killed the other over wine and then he'd taken off running, and I only lied about the ciga-

rettes, which was a mistake because she knew it from my
breath, but she forgave me and even asked me for one to
smoke after dinner, and that temptation of hers toward
my vice gave us a good laugh. Then she set about making the soup, and I have to say that she worked magic, fix-
ing a broth out of what there was, and there was nothing.
She thickened it with berries and a chewed-up rabbit bone
the kid had found half buried and dug up with his fingernails, and she gave it body with leaves, fragrant herbs, and
what was left of a can of herring, and so, with almost no
water, she made broth for the six of us, with enough left
for seconds. She used the dead soldier's helmet as a pot. We
were all very hungry, but she didn't get anxious, nor did
she rush, and she stirred the soup so much with that same
rabbit bone that it seemed like the entire world revolved
around her wrist. Without the idiots from the dam or that
fool who'd carried the water container, now that we were
only the two water owners, the driver, and the two of us
with the boy, it struck me that the group had more of a
future and, though I didn't say it out loud, I had the sen-
sation that at least when it came to this we all agreed, because, for a good long while, as she stirred and stirred the
soup with that makeshift spoon, I think we felt good and
almost like a family, despite being far away from all that
was ours and not close to anything at all.

   To sleep, we lay close to the fire, which had already sunk
to embers and could warm us without the threat of flames.

The driver was very tall, and he lay a little farther away so as not to burn his feet, and I lay close to the driver, though trying not to touch him, and she put her head on my chest, and in the triangle we made between us went the boy, and beside my wife lay the water owner's wife, and as they got along splendidly there was no problem with them being so close, and beside the water owner's wife lay her husband, the man who'd married the water without deserving it, the one who might be carrying a gun. We'd walked so much and had such a strange day that we all quickly surrendered to sleep. Through a half-opened eye, I saw the kid move and then get up, and this worried me a little, but when I heard him pee I calmed down, and I put my arm around her more tightly, and slept.

I'm not one to tell my dreams, because hearing other people's dreams strikes me as the most boring thing in the world, so let's just say that I dreamed of the soup, and around and around in the soup, and soup and more soup, and everything we'd been before burning our house seemed to fit inside that soup in the dead soldier's helmet, and there was nothing else in my dreams but the thickness of that damn soup and that's how it was until we woke.

A T DAWN, I WAS FIRST VERY GLAD TO LEAVE MY NIGHT-
mare behind, then scared to death because as soon as
I heard birds singing, I opened my eyes to a gun in my face.

It seemed that the water owner had indeed been carrying a hidden gun, but it was Julio pointing the thing at me,
Julio our boy, and he was doing it as a game, with no intention of killing me. I took the gun from him and hid it in
my trousers. It was a small weapon, an Astra, inlaid with
mother-of-pearl, an odd pistol made for the rich, a collec-

tor's item, but of the kind that never fails, limited series. I was never in the army because I wasn't drafted in my day, but I know a little about short guns, and long guns, too. Coming from the country as I do, I'm fond of shooting, not only to fell wild animals but also to chase them away, and when you're out there alone, and I was very much alone as a kid, it's better to be armed than naked.

Since the others were all sleeping and the water owner was still snoring with his mouth open, I guessed that Julio had taken the gun from him without anyone knowing. It goes without saying that I scolded the boy, gesturing severely but not raising my voice, so that I wouldn't wake the others, and then I started thinking about what to do with the damn pistol. If I gave it back to its owner, that is to say the water owner, I'd curry his favor, but I already had his favor through our wives, and if I didn't return it, I'd strip him of some power and status, because without a gun he wouldn't be able to defend the water we had left, nor could he go around giving orders with that same authoritative tone. If he got suspicious, that too could work to my advantage, and help protect my family. If he suspected the driver, he'd be left without knowing the way to the transparent city; if he suspected me, he'd be left alone with the driver without knowing who had the gun; if he was suspicious of all of us and went out alone with his wife, I'd be left with the driver and his map and the gun and without anyone to order me around—in other words, I'd become the center of our group, no one to tell me when to stop or keep going. As I considered this, the kid laughed quietly like he knew what I was thinking, and he even seemed gleeful about what his mischief had wrought. At that very moment, I decided to teach him a lesson. Sometimes, with children, there are only a few chances to teach them right from wrong, so you have to take advantage of the ones you get. Decision made, I carefully approached the water owner so as not to disturb our sleeping wives, and I woke him gently, barely touching his shoulder. Then, silently, I handed him his gun, and the man put it away and thanked me and stood up and gave me a hug. The boy Julio watched all of it without understanding a thing, and when I returned to his side I gave him an explanation that seemed, at the time, the best one. What's not right, I said, looking into his eyes, is wrong, and it never results in any good. The best way to get ahead in life, I added, is to have a clear conscience.

With the little noise we made, or perhaps because they were almost done with their own dreams, the women woke. The driver kept on snoring until the water owner roused him with the tip of his foot. When I saw the way he pushed his boot into the driver, I felt a pang of regret at having given back the gun, but I didn't regret it altogether because I was trying to teach the boy something, not to change the general order of things.

The women freshened up the way bears do, with saliva,

as what was left in the water container wasn't enough for
bathing, and, in fact, sip by little sip, the rest of it was gone.
Without water, the only things left to establish authority were the map and, of course, the gun, which just the
kid and I knew existed, besides, obviously, the man who
owned it.

As soon as we'd all stretched, we got moving again. Since
there were so few of us now, there was no need for orders.
The driver opened the map and said, this way, and that's
the way we went.

As we left the thicket of trees, the land began to slope
downward, and while the day before had been a difficult
upward climb, today's walk was happily downhill. She no
longer walked beside the water owner's wife, but with me,
arm in arm, the boy Julio fluttering around us. It was a
beautiful day, and for a while we forgot the war and everything else, and simply walked. We went a long time without water, but nobody complained, and we left the mountains behind us and reached a field so vast we couldn't see
where it ended, with grass so tall it reached our waists. She
bit into a stalk for its water and sap. I felt like a fool for being from the country and not having thought of that first.
We chewed the green grass, like cows, and we noticed, or at
least I noticed, that this strengthened our legs and cleared
the head. We were gnawing on our strange breakfast when
the patrol appeared.

First we heard the helicopter blades, and when we looked up at the cloudy sky it was already upon us, shaking the grass and blowing wind through our hair and clothes, and the women's skirts flew up almost all the way. We thought the helicopter might descend, but it didn't, and because we were watching it, we didn't see the army tank approaching, crushing the grass.

Good morning, ladies and gentlemen, said a lieutenant in uniform, the same uniform worn by my sons, belonging to our side of the war.

Good morning, we said in unison.

Where are you going? the lieutenant said, holding his machine gun up to his face, to which we responded that we were going where we'd been told to go, to the transparent city. To be honest, the water owner said it, and the rest of us just nodded. The lieutenant then asked for our papers and we handed them over. I gave him the papers for all three of us, hers, mine, and the boy's, and although his were fake, they'd been acceptable to the zone agent, all in order. The lieutenant admitted as much, and, on seeing that everything was legal and aboveboard, he relaxed a bit and lowered his weapon. The driver approached him and respectfully showed the lieutenant the map, in hopes that he might offer some suggestion. You're headed the wrong way, the lieutenant told us, you're at least thirty kilometers east of the route, and, taking out a pen, he drew the correct path on the map and then pointed in the right direction. We'd take you ourselves, he said, but there are enemies in the area and we're on a different mission.

We understood perfectly, and thanked him. As we passed the tank, she asked about our sons, but the lieutenant, a polite man, explained that the army was very big and it was impossible to know all the soldiers. The most curious thing was that when the water owner dared ask for water, the lieutenant told him that water was extremely expensive at this time because of the lack of rain and the sabotage of the wells and the price gouging of those in charge of reservoirs. Even so, and because he was a good man, he gave us a canteen and told us that if we didn't get lost on the road, that should be enough to get us to the city, parched, but alive.

The water owner's wife asked how far away we were exactly, and the lieutenant replied that at a good pace it might take the rest of the day, a good night of rest — as it was no use traveling in the dark — and one more morning. It didn't seem like enough water for so much time, but why ask for more when it wouldn't be given? He did tell us, though, of an abandoned hotel along the way where we might sleep under a roof and possibly scrounge a thing or two to eat and drink, as it hadn't been empty for very long. It was an enemy hotel, and all of this was enemy territory, so there was no need to worry about taking whatever we found. That said, his own soldiers had already sacked the place a couple of times, so we shouldn't expect to find much. That's what the lieutenant told us before turning the tank around and carrying on his patrol of the area. The helicopter hovered at a watchful distance while we talked, and I imagine it had weapons aimed at us the entire time. When the army tank left, the helicopter flew away and the grass went still and the noise stopped, and for this we were grateful, since with the lieutenant we'd had to shout to be heard.

It took us a couple of hours to get all the way across the field, and we must have gotten fleas or something because we spent the next two hours scratching ourselves incessantly. The kid Julio threw himself on the ground and rubbed himself against it like a goat, though who knows whether he did it because he itched that much or because he wanted to amuse us. If it was the latter, he was successful, as we all laughed so hard that we got even thirstier. My wife was the one who told him to stop acting like a clown. She treats him more like a son, or a nephew, while I sometimes forget myself and think he's some sort of toy, here to entertain us. She's reminded me of this, she's scolded me and rightly so, and I've had no choice but to accept it. When she scolds me, she always does it so sweetly that it's almost a pleasure, she doesn't treat me like I'm stupid but like she's concerned for me and my feelings. Especially when, like now, she has to reprimand me in front of strangers. I never hold any resentments against her, and if I get angry, which I sometimes do just like anyone else in the world, the anger fades as soon as I remember how much she's given me in life, and the little she's asked for in return.

❖

After we emerge from the large field, we see the hotel the lieutenant told us about. Though it isn't very far away, it's going to be hard to get there because it's at the top of a steep hill, with only one road. Setting foot on gravel has made me feel better; even though I'm more of a country person, I like to know where I'm headed, and roads are always a more direct route than dirt paths, above all when they aren't the dirt paths you know. As we climb, I have to take the kid into my arms because he's so tired, and I would have carried him piggyback, since that's more comfortable, if it weren't for the pain in my spine. I've got two crushed vertebrae from when I fell off the reaping machine like an idiot, out of carelessness. It doesn't bother me too much, and I'm only reminded of it when it rains or when I carry something heavy. At home she'd give me salves that did me a lot of good. Her hands are strong but soft, and she gives massages like the ones I imagine professionals give, and I say *imagine* because in all my life nobody has ever touched my back but her. It's not as if I hadn't been with other women before her, because I had, it's just that there was never affection with any of them. Before she talked to me, I was little more than a brute when it came to socializing, but I was a very diligent worker, that much I can say. At school I learned enough to read and do some arithmetic, and at thirteen my father sent me to a farm as an apprentice, and at eighteen I was already the foreman, and from then on my wife's first husband looked to me to oversee the land that later became mine. About that man, who was her husband and my boss, I can only speak well of him, as he never treated me badly and he paid me without fail and even threw in little bonuses because he was so happy with my work. He was much older than her, but he treated her well and with care, though he wasn't a husband in the sense of being a man for what a young woman needs, he couldn't give her children, nor did he try. The crueler gossips used to say that when he drank he liked to look at the boys who worked on the estate, who labored on the land or in the stables, but neither she nor I had any proof whatsoever of that. Some say that she married up, just as I did later, but in a very different way, because she was from a good name with little land, and he was the exact opposite. I had neither thing. The truth is, he died of old age, almost painlessly, and two years after his burial, more than enough time for mourning, I went up to my wife's bedroom for the first time, and two months later we married at the altar, and a short time later our first son, Augusto, was born. If you insist on doing the math, it's clear that we conceived before marriage, but I don't believe we're the first couple or the last whose desire precedes the wedding bells. Plus, our region isn't as refined as the capital, all sorts of things went on around there, everyone lived in their own way, and as long as the scandals weren't too out of control, no one caused a ruckus. There might be rumors, sure, but rumors are drowned out if you work hard and make enough noise with the hammer and anvil of your own life. And if you do hear them, you ignore them, and if for whatever reason you can't, you take out your shotgun and make them shut up. I've shut up more than one smartass without firing a single shot, just by taking my Remington on walks around the hills, or to public holidays, where everyone can see. The Remington takes six shells, and once I went to the town bar and declared that the first twelve people to question whether I had the right to be master of my land would be answered with a bullet each, and then, if the whispers continued, I'd go home for more shells and dole out more answers. Of course, nobody said a word, and I drank my wine, prouder than the captain of a ship, and after that I never returned to the bar and rarely went into town.

None of that matters anymore, the house is burned and who knows whether we'll ever set foot on our land again, and in the new city I imagine that, with people from different places living in close quarters, nobody will know anything about anyone, and there won't be any pasts to condemn or hide. She, the boy Julio, and I will be like everybody else, which will be both good and bad. I don't think it'll be hard for me, since I was born without anything to my name, but I don't know what it'll be like for her, given that she was born the heiress of a lost estate and then married into a real one. True, she's strong and has a good imagination, something I don't have, and imagination makes everything more bearable, makes you less likely to curse your circumstances. So maybe I'll be the one to struggle more with suddenly having nothing after having grown used to the good life.

When we reached the abandoned hotel, the kid was fast asleep in my arms, and she, much as she tried to hide it, was exhausted, and I, why deny it, was wiped out. The hotel was more of a spa riddled with sulfurous pools, and now that they were stagnant and deserted they smelled the way you'd imagine it smells in hell. If we were going to sleep there, we'd have to sleep on the porch, avoiding the direction of the wind; it was nauseating to step inside, so only the driver and I entered to see whether we could find any-

thing to drink or to fill our stomachs. Just as the lieutenant had said, soldiers had been through, and even a herd of
pigs couldn't have left the place in a worse state. It's star-
tling the way people treat what isn't theirs, that urge to destroy everything that many doubtlessly have inside them
but that emerges only when allowed to—when, without
authorities to keep them in line, people unleash the most
brutal parts of themselves and charge at everything in a
terrifying rage. I wanted to believe, when I saw the inside
of the hotel—the overturned tables, the shattered dishes,
the excrement, the broken windows—that my two sons
would never do anything like that, no matter how bad
the war or how soldierly they've become. You always hear
about atrocities in war zones, where the insanity of it all
gives soldiers free rein to go savage, but I want to think that
we've raised our sons to have more sense than that and to
restrain their own behavior even when nobody's control-
ling them. In any case, the driver and I searched the entire
hotel, which wasn't small, our faces covered with handker-
chiefs to ward off the stench. We looked like two bandits
from a Wild West movie, but as for stealing (though it's not
really stealing to claim abandoned things), we couldn't,
because there was nothing to take. Only a few curtains to
use as blankets for the cold, and that was it, as the mat-
tresses, and there were dozens in there, were soaked in
urine, blood, or worse. I didn't want to imagine what had
happened in there, not for a second, but I hoped the ho-

tel had been empty when the soldiers arrived, that no one was here to receive them, especially any women, since we all know what some soldiers could do to girls they find defenseless and alone.

There were no dead bodies in sight, but there was blood everywhere and there were bullet holes in the walls, like people had been shot. The driver and I sensibly agreed not to let the women and child come in, since the slightest glimpse inside this place was enough for a thousand nightmares, and in any case the stench had already made the ladies vomit the little they'd eaten in the past two days.

We went back out to the porch with our bad news, empty-handed with the exception of the curtains, which would at least make good blankets, and which were well received. It was already dark and the women were shivering, but the boy was already sleeping sweetly on the wooden porch, and it did me good to see he wasn't the fussy type, that he was a hardy kid. Nobody raised the question of food for fear of getting hungrier, but the water owner had a surprise for us that he generously shared. In his boot he'd hidden a tube of condensed milk that, though it wasn't much, helped us catch our breath and refresh our brains with sugar, which we'd sorely needed—lack of sweetness can cloud your thoughts. The bad part, of course, was that it made us all thirsty, first the ladies and then the kid, who sipped his portion while half asleep, the way kids do when they're hungry and tired at the same time.

The condensed milk paste stuck to our throats, and the little we each got from the canteen wasn't enough to relieve them, and it seemed, at least to me, that the paste didn't even reach our stomachs. With that, we went to sleep, trying not to dwell on what couldn't be helped, and dreaming — at least I was dreaming, though I think we all were — of arriving at the transparent city in the morning and, finally, drinking tons of water. She and I curled up with the boy, and she whispered words of love to me before falling asleep and said she was very proud of me, which I didn't fully understand, I couldn't quite tell what was behind it, but it made me feel hot inside and helped me close my eyes with something other than sadness, to forget for a moment the rest of my needs. It's astonishing to realize that love can nourish and calm you even in the worst of circumstances, or precisely and with good reason in the worst of circumstances. Since I don't know how to talk the way she does, and words of love don't come naturally to me, I didn't respond to her whispers. Instead, not wanting to seem less affectionate, and to make up for what was missing, I embraced her with all my strength and kissed her on the lips and stroked her hair until I heard her breathing deeply, and only when I knew she was asleep could I allow myself to drift off as well.

It must have been the end of the night, no more than an hour before dawn, when I woke to the creaking of the porch. As soon as I opened my eyes, I saw the water owners and the driver on their feet, ready to leave like robbers, quietly, trying to trick us in our sleep. They had the canteen and the map, thinking, I imagine, that the water would help them arrive in a better state, and better three than six. Knowing that the water owner was armed, that I myself had given him back the gun, it didn't occur to me to protest, and though I didn't like this dirty game, I thought that if the city was as close as the lieutenant had said, less than half a day's journey away, she and the kid and I would be perfectly able to get there on our own. If the city was big enough to take in all the evacuated regions, it would be visible from a distance, and since the lieutenant had clearly pointed east, we'd have to be idiots not to reach it. Once there, I'd find that damn water owner and settle the score, I swore this to myself as I pretended to sleep and watched from the corner of my eye as the three traitors set off, leaving us lying there without the slightest remorse. It goes without saying that I regretted giving back the gun and not using it to kill them both, the water owner and the driver —not the lady, of course, as she almost certainly wasn't to blame for anything, and even if she was, I'm not a pig and would never kill a woman. And despite their betrayal, I wouldn't have been able to kill the other two to get the canteen or the map, I don't think I could have done it, I don't have a murderer's heart, so my regret for not killing them was fake, not sincere. Sometimes, when you're gripped by rage, you think horrible things just to release them from your soul and to realize that you aren't really capable of doing them. When I arrived at the town bar that day to threaten the gossips, I didn't intend to shoot anyone; I've never harmed a human being with my own hands in my life. As a matter of fact, if I'm going to tell things the way they really happened, I showed up in the bar with my shotgun but didn't say a word or threaten anyone, and now I don't know why I exaggerated so much before. I suppose we all like to tell things in a way that makes us seem braver, even if we end up looking childish and dumb. I'm not a show-off, but sometimes, without any reason, people who lack glory go out and invent some. Basically, at the bar, I didn't say much, all I did was sit there with my shotgun — not so strange at all, as I was coming from the hunt and had partridges tied to my belt and a rabbit in my pouch — and I drank my wine, paid, and left as people whispered maliciously around me, and if I didn't return to the bar, it was out of shame, and I don't know what I was thinking with all that hot air before, when I've never been like that nor have I ever wanted to be. In the same vein, I let those three go more out of fear of the water owner's gun than any other reason, and there's no point in searching for deeper explanations. I'm not a liar by nature, and I'm no good at fooling myself. And if I have to apologize for lying, I'll do it and let that be the end of it.

My mind was going in circles and I couldn't go back to sleep. I slipped away from her and the boy, out from under the heavy curtain, and found a spot to sit and watch the sunrise. At least with this, God was generous. As the night faded I could see, from the edge of the porch and not far from the foot of the mountain, a glass dome reflecting the first rays of sun so brilliantly that you'd have to be blind not to see it. I estimated that, at a good pace, we'd be there in three hours, and I waited for my family to wake up, calmer now, eager to give them the good news as a kind of fortifying breakfast. I wasn't sure what we'd find in that city, but the people who called it transparent weren't lying, and one thing was certain, after two days of starving, it was thrilling to see.

When they woke, she and the boy stared at the dome with the same astonishment and urge to get there, and so we immediately set off toward it.

THE CITY SEEMED LARGE FROM A DISTANCE, BUT IT WAS actually even larger. And though at first it looked like a round dome, from up close we could clearly see that it was made of diamond-shaped slabs of glass or crystal affixed to the ground and placed one on top of the other to form a gigantic transparent half-sphere protecting the whole city. How something like that was built is beyond me, but it seemed — and to her, too, well read as she is — the most fabulous construction we'd ever seen or imagined, and not even in the capital, with its grand buildings and skyscrapers, had we ever known anything like it. It's hard to describe its magnitude and beauty to someone who hasn't seen it, let alone the complexity of everything beneath that dome, as it housed endless highways and blocks full of buildings and trains and tracks and markets, all of them made of glass or some other transparent material. I don't think it could really be glass or crystal, since either would have broken under all the weight, and yet, without knowing the first thing about architecture or the science behind this vast, gleaming city, I can't find a better way to describe it.

Everything was transparent, and behind one block of homes you could see the next one and the next, and everything looked jumbled together but also clean and orderly, and this city didn't have or didn't seem to have any shadows, hiding places, or corners the light didn't reach. And if the dome that protected everything was made of diamond-shaped glass, inside everything was also built out of transparent diamond-shaped slabs, like a hive inside a hive inside a hive, and within that clarity the people looked like industrious bees moving here and there, going about their affairs. The entrance to the city was a wide, six-lane highway, but with very little traffic, none actually, so you might believe that nobody left the city and few entered it. I wondered how so many people could be sustained with-

out trucks transporting food, without the coming and going of goods that happens in all cities and ports and even
in small towns, and if it was possible that all the things you
needed to live there were already inside. There also wasn't
an airport in sight, or any trains arriving or departing, only
the train that ran inside the dome, which was like an ant-
hill you find under a rock, built meticulously from the
inside and without any outside help. Nobody was on the
highway except for the three of us, on foot, and in the long
hour it took us to arrive we didn't meet a soul or see a single vehicle enter or exit the transparent city. The boy said
nothing, as usual, but as we got closer his eyes lit up with
enthusiasm, though at his young age he couldn't possibly
understand how remarkable the place really was. The poor
boy may have thought, with the little he likely knew of
the world, that there were similar cities elsewhere, but we
knew that wasn't true, that not even in books could you
find photos of anything like this in any foreign country,
nor on the moon, nor on other planets, nor had we heard
a traveler ever tell of a city as clear, huge, and monumen-
tal as this one.

The entire city was open, since the base was made of the
pointed ends of thousands of transparent diamond-shaped
blocks, and it didn't seem to be fenced in, nor did we see any
armed guards. However, at the main entrance, or what we
assumed was the main entrance, since the only highway led

us straight to it, we encountered a checkpoint where two uniformed agents asked for our papers. We gladly handed them over, and they, after examining the documents carefully and verifying the official seals, offered us a formal yet encouraging greeting: welcome to the transparent city.

◇◇◇

If it hadn't been for the kid, I wouldn't have noticed the only terrible thing we saw on our way in. Julio was the one who pointed out the bodies of the water owners, husband and wife, hanging from a post — more of a tube — made of crystal or glass. They dangled face-down like two ominous fruits just behind the border checkpoint.

It was obvious that they were dead, and a coarse paper sign had been sewn onto each of their chests, with a single handwritten word: TRAITOR.

She covered her eyes in horror, and covered the kid's eyes too. And I stood there staring, stunned, not sure what to say. I wasn't too fond of the man, and I think with good reason, but the sight of them made me realize how things were dealt with in the new world, and I told her and the boy that until we understood how justice worked here, we should tread very carefully.

Once inside, however, we were attended to — rather coldly, it's true, but when it came down to it, they did meet our most urgent needs. The first thing they did, after verifying and stamping our papers one more time, was take us on foot to a kind of refugee camp where there were many people like us, recent arrivals, battered and hungry. The tents didn't really look like tents, because instead of being made of canvas, like the tents I knew, they were made of an exquisite cloth, firmer yet more transparent than gauze, and you could see everything going on inside, including the showers, which made us feel embarrassed for the boy but also for ourselves, all those naked men and women in plain sight. It seemed that modesty didn't matter here, and we'd have to get used to it. Where there's no modesty, there's no shame, my dear mother used to say.

Before we headed to the showers, we were given plenty of water to drink, and fruit and bread and cold cuts on small plates so we'd satisfy our hunger without overeating, and chocolate so we could regain our energy, and hot coffee, which we'd sorely missed during the journey. The people there spoke so little to us that I wondered whether they were foreigners, but others who were eating beside us said no, they were the last of ours. I didn't understand what *the last of ours* meant until later, when I learned about it in pre-education classes. We were also referred to as the last suspects, as it seemed that, according to those who taught us, beyond the city we were all allies now and there was nothing but peace in the world, and inside the city anyone who didn't do things the way they were told would be considered an enemy and adorn the post at the main gate. On the other hand, there was no need to worry about odors or rotting, because they had a cleaning method that made it so that nothing smelled anywhere in the city, not the living or the dead. It was called crystallization, and it was applied to you in your first shower, and one thing was for certain: you'd never smell your own body again, or the bodies of others. Not even by sticking our noses right on each other's skin could she and I recognize our scents, which of course is very clean but also very odd, because there is no smell like the smell of your woman, and every person is accustomed to their own smell and the smell of the person they love, so much so that until smell is snatched away from you, you can't realize how different you'll feel without it.

In the city, everything was crystallized and nothing smelled. People didn't sweat or cry, no liquid left the body except urine, which also didn't smell, something to be thankful for, considering that my job was at the recycling

and waste management center, which means that I managed urine and feces, and none of it smelled, and the sci-
entist who found a way to do this should be given all the
prizes in the world, since feces without the odor is not so
different from, or more distressing than, mud.

But one thing at a time. With all the surprises I found
in the glass city, I'm getting things jumbled and losing the
thread. When we finished our showers and our crystallization, we received clean clothes. Not uniforms, but normal shirts and trousers made of light cloth, and they let us
choose our colors. There was no problem finding the right
size, as there was enough clothing in this place to dress an
army, though, let's be honest, it would be an army of civilians. All very light, made of linen or cotton, no wool
or leather, as the temperature was mild and consistent
and always controlled, and there was no cold or heat, and
there was even a gentle, odorless breeze that was awfully
pleasant.

Everything was perfect and monitored in the city, or so
it appeared. Of course, we'd have to see how things un-
folded, because no place, no matter where you go, is perfect, and we should thank God that that's the way it is. Or
maybe that's just me, I've always been slow to trust, or
maybe fearful. She always criticizes me for this.

Our first home, to name it in some way, was the arrival
camp; we spent our first two nights there, in reasonable

comfort, with individual beds that were arranged in rows of ten in a large common dormitory. We had to adapt to not sleeping in each other's arms, as she and I always had before, and also to the annoying sleep masks, since it wasn't only the weather that was constant, but also the light, as the transparent city never went dark. I'm no doctor, but I know enough to think it can't be good for you psychologically, that since we're all used to daytime and nighttime, this approach would surely have disastrous consequences, and I wondered why they did it, whether they wanted us to go mad, which didn't really make sense, because aside from the light they took very good care of us, as if out of real concern for our well-being.

The kid was the least bothered by the eye masks, and he kept sleeping deeply as always, while it took her and me longer to get to sleep those first nightless nights and without each other's embrace, but she calmed me by saying that we'd surely end up adapting because everything in life can be adapted to when you don't have any other choice. We didn't make any friends in the arrival camp, but we spoke to a few people from our region who'd reached the city before us in what had started out as the third bus. They were as lost as we were, taking whatever came without much protest or enthusiasm. Since everything was new and different, it was hard to know what to think. One can imagine that in such an organized place everything is optimally ar-

ranged, so it didn't seem right to complain about what we
didn't yet understand, and I think that others in the arrival
camp, and of course she and I, preferred to simply wait and
keep our judgment at bay.

Aside from that, as long as we didn't leave the camp
until the crystallization process and its accompanying
quarantine were complete, we were free enough to chat,
move about, play with the boy, and do what we wanted,
though while we were stuck in that place, there wasn't
much we could do. They did give us reading material so
we wouldn't get bored. No newspapers, no magazines,
but books of every kind, not only novels but also techni-
cal manuals, science books, and books about medicine, en-
gineering, and gardening. There was something for everyone, for all interests. She picked up a pirate novel, *Treasure
Island,* which she'd also had at home and which she liked
a great deal, and she also reached for a Bible. I'm less of
a reader, but as time kept passing I ended up with a big
encyclopedia of world wildlife that had beautiful drawings of all the planet's animals and had the added bene-
fit of entertaining the boy. Julio had a great time with
that book, he never got bored of looking at it, and when
he was given paper and pens he started drawing animals
from it, one by one, from the very first page. They didn't
come out badly, the caretakers praised his drawings, and
within two days the kid won more attention and affection

from the staff than she or I or anyone else in the dormitory. He was the only kid among us and he brought us all joy. When we left the camp, we were told we could keep the books, and Julio was thrilled because there were still a thousand or more animals for him to draw, and I wondered whether he'd be able to do all of them, as sometimes children enjoy something for a while and then forget about it. That's not what happened. That volume showed us that our child, for he was ours now, was incredibly tenacious and hardworking when something interested him. She and I were very happy to see that Julio was talented and diligent, and we thought that no matter how life turned out in this city, those qualities would surely help him a great deal. We showered three times a day, for the crystallization, and in two days I got wet more than I used to in an entire week, because I'd always bathed every other day, unlike her, she'd scrubbed herself daily. Julio was given a water gun so he wouldn't get bored with all the showering, and he had a great time wetting all our asses, and when I say all, I mean all the residents of the dormitory, because we all showered together, men, women, and children, though, as I said, the only kid among us was our own. It's a bit shocking at first to see strangers or people you hardly know as naked as they were when God sent them into the world, but you get used to it by the third shower, since, in the end, although some of us have more flesh in this or that place and others have less, we're basically all the same. All the walls in the city were transparent and there was daylight around the clock, so it made no sense to go around worrying about what you could hide, or to feel any shyness or shame.

THINGS WEREN'T SO BAD FOR US AT THE ARRIVAL CAMP, but as is logical and easy to understand for anyone attached to their things, we were happy to be given our own house.

In reality, it wasn't a house at all, but a small apartment on one of the hundreds of transparent city blocks. It had a kitchen, bathroom, and bedroom for the three of us, with three armchairs, one for each, and a sofa and a table big enough to eat on. Everything was kept clean, as the city took care of that, and it was also, as I've already said, transparent, so that if you looked right or left or up or down you could see all the neighbors, which was strange but also very entertaining—at least at first, as later, since everyone does more or less the same things, I'm guessing it'll end up as mundane and boring as spending your whole life staring into a mirror. There was no television, not in our apartment or in any other, nor a radio or anything noisy, and anyway, sound couldn't have been a problem since, though the walls were very thin, they were also soundproof, and though we could see everything, we heard nothing. When it came to talking, at least, we had all the privacy we wanted. Everything else had to be done in plain sight. Naturally, the first time you answer the call of nature in such conditions it's almost impossible to focus, and what's more, shit falls through glass tubes that move through the building from top to bottom, which, as much as it cracks up the kid and endlessly amuses him, is beyond bizarre. But there's no odor; one thing for another, I guess. In the world we lived in before, shit was less visible but it smelled a lot worse. I realize I might be going on too long about topics that aren't very important and are vulgar and unsavory, but, as I mentioned, this ended up being my line of work, so that's why it stands out in my mind.

I was informed of my job at the same time we were placed in our home, and they told me where to report for duty. That same afternoon, after lunch—they had left food for us in the transparent refrigerator — I was escorted to the recycling and waste management center. They weren't going to lead me to work by the hand every day, but since I didn't know my way around the city yet, a kind woman brought me to my workplace, explaining everything with great patience and giving me a map so I could get there by myself in the future. The map was unnecessary, as the city was perfectly organized and full of signs, and to get lost on these streets you'd have to be stupid, something I've never been. Also, the center wasn't far from us, just three blocks away. In this city, according to the woman, nobody worked far from their block so as not to waste time, which seemed reasonable to me.

Since it couldn't be otherwise, I started at the bottom, at the very bottom, in what was called the white basement, which was where all the city's shit ended up. The basement was enormous, and tractors moved around dragging wheeled containers by chains, and inside those containers were large rectangular glass boxes resembling coffins, all full of feces, forming what from a distance looked like huge worms of shit. They gave me a jumpsuit that fit me perfectly and explained the work I'd be doing. It consisted simply of driving those tractors, which weren't so different from the ones on the farm, and dragging one of those worms from door to door. The first door led to the room where excrement was received and packaged, and the second door, on the other end of the white basement, led to the recycling center. There, other workers would unload the containers and do whatever was done with the feces, which was something incredible, because they turned the shit into fertilizer and fuel and construction materials. Apparently, the glass or crystal was made of natural polycarbons extracted from shit. Urine was distilled in a similar basement and turned into drinking water. It was a bit disgusting when you thought about it, but it was also logical and, of course, practical, since that way the city could provide for itself and literally didn't lose a drop. There wasn't a single gram of waste that didn't get put to use. I must add that the city's running water tasted just like water from a mountain stream, and the first sip of such clean, pure, fresh water quenched your thirst and erased any squeamishness.

I received general instructions and jumped right in, not asking about the pay, or about vacation days, or anything of the sort, as I guessed that such a modern and scientifically advanced place would have worked out all the details. If they could do what they did with shit and urine, what wouldn't these good people do with everything else.

Since we were given our food and clothes and even books, and I hadn't seen a single store where I could buy things, I imagined that maybe there wasn't any money in this city, not a bad idea, since it removes greed and ambition and prevents people from envying what they see as greener grass. The more time I spent in the transparent city, and the more I discovered, the more intelligently organized it all seemed, and though it's never easy for someone to leave behind everything they've known and adapt to new surroundings, I found it hard to complain. Whether or not I liked the work I'd been assigned, or the home they gave us, or not being able to smell my wife the way I used to, was all beside the point, because the most urgent thing in a situation like this one, I think, is to settle in as soon as possible and not go around splitting hairs. The work wasn't very hard, and we took a snack break and were even allowed to chat for a while with our coworkers, whom I decided to refer to that way from the moment I arrived, acting friendly to make it clear that there would be no problems or fights with me and that I was more than willing to be one among many. As soon as I started talking to them I realized that we were all more or less in the same situation, that each of us had been evacuated from some other part of the country, and that they also didn't know anything about the war; they received no news at all. I couldn't help wanting to know what they'd heard before arriving in the city, since my two boys were still at the front and I had no idea how the hell we were going to find them or whether they'd be able to find us. One man told me that according to the last thing he'd heard, the war was over, and we hadn't won it, and our soldiers were probably imprisoned or dead. I told them we had seen soldiers some kilometers from here, but they said those must have been enemy troops, to which I replied that it wasn't possible because they spoke our language. And then another man explained that many of ours had changed sides and that they weren't ours anymore, but rather part of the enemy. What's certain is that I never found out whether my sons were already dead, or imprisoned, or whether they were, like the ones we saw, enemies —although, when you thought about it, if the war was over, then they weren't enemies anymore. From the beginning, I've never understood this war, how it started or why exactly we were fighting. I left the conversation not knowing if I should be more or less worried than before about Augusto and Pablo, and I asked God only that they be alive and whole. And I didn't know whether to tell her all the things I'd heard, as I didn't want to frighten her. If the provisional government we believed to be ours actually belonged to the enemy, and we were no longer ourselves but part of them, we'd have to be very careful about what our children now were and where they were fighting, if they were fighting, and what side they were currently on. Basically, it all seemed like a big mess and something we should talk over calmly when we knew more. We'd have to demand or request, to the extent that we could, information about the boys once we had a better sense of the government overseeing us, and without bothering anyone, that's for sure. Given what happened to the water owners, we'd already seen how these people deal with dissent.

Speaking of which, it was rumored that the water own-

ers kept their pulse system active all this time, and that
they'd given WRIST detailed accounts of our group's move-
ments, and that they came to the transparent city with the
intention to act as spies, report on what happened here,
and do everything they could to support cells of resistance.
And that this, and no other reason, was why they'd been
hung face-down. In this city where everything could be
seen, the only thing that was forbidden was precisely that:
hiding or spying, because, really, why bother spying when
everything was already visible and all intentions were crystal clear and radiant. I didn't know whether to believe it or
not, but as I've already said, it didn't seem like a good idea
to ask too many questions.

Regretfully, I had to put our soldier sons out of my
mind as soon as the snack break was over, as my coworkers had prepared a hazing for me, and when I got back to
the tractor they started pummeling me with balls of shit
that smelled of nothing, and they laughed so hard at their
own prank that I ended up laughing too, and I threw some
nice balls of my own back at them, and if it hadn't been
shit, I might have thought we looked just like kids having a snowball fight. After a while, the supervisor showed
up, and we stopped playing around and went back to
work. The supervisor wasn't upset, and told me this sort
of prank was normal with new hires, as a way of getting
to know each other and dropping the formalities, creating
a bond, since without bonds, work could end up monoto-

nous, boring, and interminable, and that, aside from this, the people of the white basement were fantastic coworkers and I shouldn't worry, that once I'd gotten past the hazing, I was one of them and there would be no more pranks but a great deal of respect and support for whatever I needed, as well as other kinds of jokes, ones that bring you joy but don't get you dirty.

I couldn't have cared less about the hazing, in fact I'd had a good time, so the supervisor's reaction, with all his careful explanations, seemed exaggerated. After all, that sort of thing between men and women who work and sweat together, even if the sweat doesn't stink, is completely harmless, but the supervisor was the kind of snooty guy who loved to explain the obvious. He was also, to be sure, very polite and well mannered.

At the end of the workday I left my tractor in the garage with all the others — there must have been two hundred of them — and headed to the showers with my coworkers. There we removed the remains of all that shit that didn't smell but still clung like any ordinary shit, and then we emerged fresh, clean, and crystallized.

WHILE I WAS SATISFIED WITH HOW THINGS WERE GOING, she was enthusiastic. It's also true that her job was better than mine, but I'd expected that, since she was more educated, imaginative, and talented than me.

She was given, no more and no less, an entire section of the public library, which, considering her love of books, was the best thing they could have done. Since she was a girl, she'd dreamed of a life like this one — surrounded by stories, some real and others imagined, and full of knowl-

edge, and thoughts, and so many things to learn and enjoy
—but instead she'd found herself sentenced to the constant mundane demands of farming, land, and livestock.
She told me that I'd been a great help to her on that front,
but that now she could finally do something that she truly
loved and had been born to do. I was delighted to see her
so happy, and any worries I had were purely small-minded,
springing from the idea that this life of books that stirred
her so much would leave her with little use for me, but
she, as always, reassured me the instant she saw my unease, saying that she was eager to share all the new things
she learned with me, and though we no longer had a farm
or land to care for, I could always take care of her in other
ways, with attention and affection, and she would certainly
need those for the rest of her life, and when the boys returned I'd have to take care of all of them, Augusto, Pablo,
Julio, and her, and keep being the guide and beacon of the
family. I really liked that part about the guide and beacon,
because a man likes to know that he's counted on for important things, and I didn't want to say a word to her about
my serious concern over our soldier sons. I decided to save
that conversation for later, when we were more settled and
less disoriented.

Now that she was pleased with her job and I was satisfied with mine and we were waiting on news about our
sons at war and about the war itself, the only worry I had
left was what the plan would be for the kid, Julio, and

to make sure that he too was taken care of and had his needs met. And in this matter, the people of the transparent city, or whatever government there was, really did amaze us with their foresight and efficiency. If we thought things had been well laid out for us, the adults, where to begin to describe the exquisite way they dealt with children, who were more or less the city's royalty, or, as they put it—and with good reason, these people didn't speak just to hear their own voices—the true promise of the future. At first they left Julio at home, to rest after the journey and give him time to adjust so that he'd be prepared for all the good new things that awaited him, but very soon he'd start school, they told us, since education is essential for a child and can't be delayed. And they'd give us both permission to miss work so we could accompany him and have everything explained to us. Full of this hope, the three of us sat down at our table for our first dinner in our own home in the new city. The crystal refrigerator contained all the necessities for the day: breakfast, lunch, dinner, and a snack for the kid, since she and I received snacks at work. There was nothing else in there. The food was prepared according to each person's needs, taking into account age, weight, and type of employment, and whatever they gave you was what there was to eat, no more no less, not because they wanted to bore us but because it was the healthiest option. Rather than letting people eat what wasn't good for them, they prepared an appropriate diet so you could feel good, strong and healthy, and save on trips to the doctor. The doctors of the transparent city put more of their energy and effort into prevention than into cures, rather than the other way around, as it used to be in the rest of the world, outside the dome. We learned all of this by reading the manuals next to the fridge, because that's how it was, either they patiently explained things to you or they left you a manual so you could see that nothing was ever done on a whim and everything had its reasons.

After dinner, the three of us sat on the sofa to read for a while, she with her books and Julio and I with our animal encyclopedia. I was the first to get sleepy, and I went to bed wearing my eye mask, which I was getting used to. She tucked the kid into his cot across the room and then curled up beside me. We kissed each other affectionately and went to sleep. For a moment, I wondered what we'd do if we wanted to fuck, what with the boy in the same room as us and everyone else watching through the glass walls, but I supposed they must have thought of this too and that maybe we'd have to go to a place designed expressly for that purpose, a kind of love room, or maybe we'd have to do it very discreetly under the sheets. There were no blankets because, with the temperature perfect in our home and throughout the city, there was no need for them.

Sometimes it rained, of course, but not inside the city,

only beyond it, and it was strange to see the raindrops striking the dome without hearing any sound, and the light inside the city kept on as that beautiful midday light that shone and never changed, not in the daytime or at night or during storms. After a few days here, you didn't even glance at the sky anymore, why bother when what happened out there had nothing to do with the climate inside.

⸭

That night I slept well and dreamed that I was hunting with my boys, that we were killing an enormous wild boar. If I missed anything in the transparent city, it was my sons and my shotguns and going hunting in the hills, but so what, I already missed those things before, ever since the war began spreading to our region and the noise and flashing of bombs made all the animals flee. Maybe, over time, Augusto and Pablo would come back and the creatures would return to their forests and they'd let us go out hunting somewhere nearby. Nobody had said we were prisoners or that it was dangerous or forbidden to go out, although to be fair, we hadn't asked. Once you've been taken from your house and put in a line and transported to another place, you get used to not asking questions, to avoid making things worse. When it comes down to it, we saw the water owners hanging face-down as soon as we arrived, and since then it's been clear to me that it's better to be on these people's good side than their bad.

When the woman arrived to take us to see the school, the three of us were already showered and dressed, and had had our breakfast. The people here are extremely punctual, so it's best not to keep anybody waiting. The stroll through the city was even shorter than my walk to work, and the lady told us that the boy would go to school by himself from this day forward, that all the children went to school on their own because there was no danger on these streets, and furthermore, it helped them start taking responsibility for themselves. The truth is that there weren't many vehicles, and they were used only to transport goods. Nobody had a car, nor was there any need for one, since you could get wherever you had to go on foot or by public transportation, which was a subway system, a gorgeous crystal train that you could see through the transparent streets. Julio, of course, was crazy about the crystal train and wouldn't stop pointing at it and staring. We explained to the lady that Julio never spoke, but that he seemed to understand everything perfectly, and that he was neither deaf nor stupid. The lady told us that this was no problem at all, that there were also blind children and developmentally delayed ones at the school, and that all the kids were educated according to their needs and strengths. She added that Julio seemed particularly sharp and intelligent, and she was sure he had great potential and a bright future ahead of him, all of which made us feel proud, even though the kid wasn't really ours and therefore couldn't have inherited those qualities from us.

At the school, I let her do the talking, since she was more sophisticated and refined than me. I could see it was a lovely place and all the teachers seemed great and the students wonderfully well behaved, saying good morning when you passed them in the hall and stopping politely for other kids to pass. They also played and sang and climbed the leafy trees: there were pear trees, apple trees, orange trees, all of them laden with fruit, and also pines and large, strong elms with branches the kids could climb. It looked nothing like the school back in our town, it even had a pool and a few sports facilities like in the old Olympics. I'd never seen anything like it in my life, and when they'd shown us everything, and after we wished Julio good luck for his first day of school, she and I went off to work, talking nonstop about the wonders we'd just seen, both of us overjoyed to know that our Julio would be in good hands.

⬩⬩⬩

I left her at the library, a noble, elegant building full of books, obviously, and with people inside who read at adjoining tables. I'd never seen so many people reading at the same time, nor had she, which was why her eyes lit up at the sight of it, and she told me again how much she loved her job. I watched her enter through the glass wall and was surprised at the warmth with which her coworkers greeted her, considering she'd only just started. They hugged and kissed her when she arrived, particularly this one young man who was quite handsome, the prissy type, I disliked him as soon as I laid eyes on him, and I thought his attentions toward my wife were going too far, but since I was in a hurry I tried to put it out of my mind, and I left for the recycling and waste management center to do what was mine to do.

I didn't like leaving her in the company of that good-looking librarian, and in other circumstances I would have taken her out of there that very instant, but in this new world I would have ended up looking like a boor, so it wasn't a good move. Sometimes you have to wait for things to unfold, even though you already sense what's going to happen, because if you don't, people will call you crazy.

❖

My workday was identical to the one before, except for the hazing and my joining the union. When the union people came up to me during the snack break I didn't know who they were, but my coworkers immediately explained that joining was a free and personal choice, it was very convenient to sign up, and at this site, at least, all the workers were union members. The union people then sat down with me, and as I ate they told me about how the labor system worked here, which interested me enormously, since I still didn't understand what government ruled over this business or over the city, let alone how everything was organized, and I'm not stupid enough to think that things worked so efficiently on their own, as if by magic. In my previous life, I'd never been the sort of man to get involved in organizations or join forces with others, whether to defend myself or to attack anyone, and I always preferred to take care of myself on my own. When I was working as a laborer I never trusted anyone much, not my coworkers nor my foremen, and I learned that everything is achieved through effort and you earn respect by breaking your back, not by whining. As a foreman, I looked out for the owners' interests without exploiting the people beneath me, and when I ended up as the owner, running things on her behalf, I tried to look out for our interests and was demanding but fair, and if I had to reward someone's effort, that's what I did, and if I had to get rid of some lazybones or thief, I didn't hesitate. But that was on the estate, where there's always an owner, and here there were no owners, or so I was told, we all worked for ourselves and therefore we should be the ones making decisions. Any profits belonged to the whole city, and people did their duty for the common good, not just for themselves. Nor was there any salary in the usual sense, or, as I'd already figured from the absence of stores on the streets, anything to buy, since the city administered the essentials to each person, and even whims and entertainments were provided by the city, that is to say, by the city dwellers, by us. From what I could gather, there wasn't a boss or president or king around here either, and nobody ranked above or below anyone else. I asked them what happened to those who decided not to join the union, and they said, nothing, it was a respected and respectable option, but barely anyone took it because it meant getting shut out of decision-making, and therefore, those who weren't part of unions lived outside the law, shirking their obligation to participate in shaping the common destiny.

I barely understood what was being said, and because of my innate distrust I suspected there had to be something fishy going on and it couldn't possibly all be as fair and aboveboard as they'd described it to be, unless the people of the transparent city were of a very different kind than the ones I'd known outside, and since that's not possible — if I know anything at all it's that there are no other types of people than people, and anywhere you go they're all the same — I signed the papers and joined the union without much enthusiasm. I was extremely careful, that's for sure, so they wouldn't notice anything, and I kept my thoughts and fears to myself and signed. Of course I signed. I saw no other choice. When you're the last to arrive somewhere, you can't go around shaking things up. Still, I decided that over the long haul I'd look for one of those people who wasn't in a union, to see how they described their work experience. It had to be different in some way.

The union people clasped my hands warmly and left, and I finished my snack and returned to my tractor. Every day I dragged the same number of containers full of shit at the same automated speed, so there was little to do well or poorly, no room to improve, no way to do it more or less skillfully or with better or worse luck, which became tiring and, most importantly, offered no motivation. One thing I forgot to ask the union people was whether it was possible to choose your line of work or whether you had to accept what you were assigned, whether you could get promoted or change your post at some point, or whether this dragging worms of shit at the same pace was going to be the rest of my life. Back when I took care of the land and livestock, whether as an employee or an employer, I at least got to see the sky, and if there was no rain I waited for it, and if there was a lot of rain and everything flooded we reached for buckets and drained the place and put out sandbags to protect the orchards and the fields, and if we had a good horse we raised it affectionately until the day we sold it, and if a horse fell ill we shot it, and if wolves came for the chickens we took out the shotgun, let's go, there are things to do and we know how to do them, and luck and profits both depended on you. Here, as far as I could see, it didn't matter much whether it was me or the next guy steering the tractor, and there wasn't anything in the sky either to suggest how the day would go, or the month, the profits, the harvest.

◇◇◇◇

At the end of the workday, after a thorough shower, I went for a walk before returning home. I still didn't know the

city very well, as was to be expected, but since it was hard
to get lost, I decided to explore. All things considered, I'd
spent little time alone since we'd arrived, and even less time
seeing things for myself, without someone constantly explaining. So I wanted to be a bit of a tourist, and, why deny
it, it struck me that there might be a bar somewhere where
I could find a cold beer or a glass of wine, since nothing of
the sort had been placed in our fridge. I took everything
in with great interest, and it was, of course, a very well-
kept and beautiful city, organized like nothing I'd ever seen
before, but also much of it was the same. There were the
same buildings on every street, and the people dressed neither exactly alike nor differently, always wearing shirts and
trousers made of light fabrics that differed only in color,
the same thing on men and women, as I hadn't seen skirts
around at all, and that was a bit of a shame, not being able
to see women's legs. What was strange, or at least seemed
strange to me — no, absolutely bizarre — was that the
women were covered up on the street but when you looked
in their homes you could see them stark naked through
the glass, whether they were in the shower, undressing, or
in the bathroom, or simply because some of them felt like
doing exercises wearing little or nothing inside their crystal apartments. In a short while you saw more people just
as God sent them into the world than you would have seen
in an entire lifetime elsewhere. And yet, as I said, on the
street everyone was conservatively dressed, like they were

trying not to call attention to themselves. Overall, these people's idea of modesty was downright nuts.

That's what I was thinking about, as well as where to find a goddamn bar around here, when I ran into a familiar face. It was the zone agent, and while I never had any special fondness for the man, I was moved to see someone from my old region, which, although we'd left it only a few days before, already seemed like another lifetime and another world. The zone agent was also pleased when he recognized me, and we embraced each other, just like that, spontaneously. He immediately said that this chance meeting called for a drink, and to me this sounded like heaven's bells and I admitted that I'd already been wandering for a while in search of a bar. Done, he said, and he took me to a place that could have passed for the most average everyday pub in any town if it hadn't been made of crystal. As soon as we entered, we were served ice-cold beers, and although it had no label, it was the most delicious beer I'd ever had, or at least that's how it tasted to me, maybe because I'd been starting to fear that the people of this city were not only weird, but also sober. But no, not at all, the beer was delicious and free and there was as much as you could drink, and the bar was lively, with men and women happily chatting, laughing, and joking around. A bar the way God intended. How the zone agent and I laughed! The fact that I didn't fall off my stool more than once was a sheer miracle. Back in our region, with the whole business of our transfer and the war going on all around us, I'd never realized how witty this guy was. He apologized for his behavior before, explaining, though he didn't have to, that the seriousness of the situation and the responsibilities of his role had made him more reserved, but in reality he was a very cheerful man, friendly and sincere. As well as funny. And then some: he must have rattled off a hundred jokes. I'm terrible with jokes and can never pull off the delivery, but he told me one about a man who comes home to find his wife in bed with a horse which almost split me in two with laughter. I wish I could remember it, because it was juicy and in the end the horse could talk and turned out to be a lawyer for I don't know what fancy university and I don't know what other craziness, all of it hilarious. On the fifth beer, as often happens, while talking about the region and what had happened to the things that once were ours, we suddenly became more serious and even a little sad.

I guessed that he, as a zone agent, or a former zone agent, must know more than me about how things were going, so I started plying him for information, and the man, who was already treating me like a close friend, opened right up and, if he had been holding anything back, I couldn't tell, nor did he give me any reason to doubt his word. It's odd to see what connects people from the same region when they find themselves together in a foreign place. The two of us, I think, confessed more to each other over the course of those five pints of beer than I, for one, had wanted to confess to myself ever since we were informed of the evacuation and I had gone along without the slightest complaint.

He told me how hard it had been for him to get people out of the region, and, above all, to leave all the people whose papers the provisional government had not approved to the enemy's mercy. The man almost burst into tears as he recalled the gypsy women and children, or that suspicious pair he'd been ordered not to include in the rescue. I took advantage of this soul-baring moment to ask him about the water owners and confessed how surprised I'd been to see them hanging face-down at the city gates, despite the fact that during our brief trip together they'd acted miserably, and I also mentioned the sedition rumors that hounded them. He told me that those two deserved their fate, as in the region they'd been notorious for profiteering off water without a care for the town's thirst, and that they'd tried to shrink their own reservoir to raise the price when the provisional enemy government took over the region and then the whole country. And as for the activated WRIST, that was anything but a rumor, and they'd been bad news, trying to enter the city like two Trojan horses. He added, however, that it had turned his stomach too to see them hanging there, especially her, even though he'd been the one to write the incriminating report that led to their deaths. I could see that this man had a good heart and hadn't enjoyed taking on a role he hadn't chosen, which had forced him to commit so many cruelties.

It was also clear that he had no decision-making power in the government, and he had no choice but to carry things out to the letter. He also talked about his fear of disobeying orders, since, he told me, firing squads awaited any one of us, including him, who tried to resist or even remotely question the evacuation plan. It seemed that this had happened throughout the country, as the war had clearly been lost a long time ago and the relocation plans had been under way, without anyone knowing, for over a year, and the army had quietly prepared accordingly. As for whether we were now part of what we used to call the enemy, he confirmed that yes, it was true, but that this information had been kept carefully hidden to avoid uprisings among patriots, in case there were any, and that the provisional government was really a faction of the permanent government, which had betrayed our flag to make a pact with the enemy and negotiate terms of defeat and ensuing occupation. He also told me, and this was really a surprise, that our country had actually been the aggressor in this war and that the rest of the world, whom we called our enemies, were in fact allies for freedom, and it was our country that had acted in bad faith from the beginning, disregarding borders and forcibly annexing islands in the sea to the north and building settlements on stolen land in neighboring countries of the delta. Ultimately, if the whole question of the war were divided, for the sake of simplicity, into aggressors and victims, or, more simply, into good guys and bad guys, we were the bad guys. He briefly described the great crimes against humanity our army had committed, the death squads in refugee camps, the expulsion of dissidents, the systematic persecution of gypsies, the merciless bombing of civilians, the rapes, the mutilations, the common graves.

It pained me to hear all this, and I wished I hadn't let my sons go off to war, and I was enraged to have realized this too late, to know that I'd swallowed every bit of cursed propaganda they'd served up to us without resistance. I was repulsed, I felt it in the pit of my stomach, when you eat garbage you vomit garbage. I thought of the stupid pride I'd felt for my sons' medals, how they could be dead now, or behind bars, and all for a bad cause, and I regretted that I'd been born, first of all, and second of all I regretted being born such a fool, here in this time and place. At that point the former zone agent recognized my sadness and tried to lift my spirits by saying that we'd all been duped, that I shouldn't blame myself, that they'd lied skillfully to all of us and the lie had seemed so perfect that anyone who didn't believe it would have been called crazy. This raised my spirits somewhat, but in the end each of us has the ability to think for ourselves, and I cursed myself for not having done so more. If I had done so, he said, If I'd truly doubted the effective state propaganda of the time, they would have shot me for sure and my sons and wife would have joined me in a common grave without a cross in sight. With that, the former zone agent had me more convinced, and I really did find some comfort, or at least something real behind which I could hide and comfort myself, since it's all very well to rebel against something bad because of your ideas or courage or beliefs, but for no reason in the world should an honorable man put his loved ones in danger.

After everything I've described, as you can imagine, the conversation had taken a sour turn, and there was no trace of the laughter we'd shared a few minutes before, but keeping in mind that the beer was free, we did what we could to avoid leaving the crystal bar looking like people walking out of a funeral, or worse, like the gravediggers themselves, as this was the state we were in after discussing so many tragedies and facing so much heartbreak. Like an idiot, I asked him to tell me the joke about the horse again, the one where the horse was a lawyer and some poor man found him in bed with his wife, and it goes without saying that the second time around, as always happens, it wasn't half as funny and even struck me as in bad taste, almost painful. Sometimes when the magic is lost and the situation has degenerated the most sensible thing to do is throw in the towel, but that usually happens as the night's about to end — and night is just a figure of speech here, because night never falls in this damn city — and you rally like your life depends on it, and the last beers are poured, the ones that'll end up giving you a joyless hangover, the ones that in truth don't do anything for you, and if they do something, it's make your woman angry and give her a reason to scold you.

In the end, we left there stumbling, or almost stumbling, and were immature enough to piss on the street, which didn't absorb a thing since it was made of glass or crystal, so it all stayed there where anyone could slip and fall, a little puddle, shameful to see. People were watching, in fact, since it couldn't be any other way in a transparent city without night, and they scowled at us, and once again I felt a terrible unease, the way I'd felt every time I'd gotten drunk in my old life. Back then I couldn't drink and walk in a straight line either, couldn't be like those people who hold their liquor, though to be honest I've never met a person like that in my life.

Despite the miserable way our night had ended, we parted ways with great affection, the former zone agent and I, and we swore to do it again. We didn't exchange phone numbers because my apartment didn't have a telephone and it seemed his didn't either. We did, however, agree that we must have dinner together on Sunday, and as soon as we said this I realized despite my sorry state that I didn't know what day it was, nor whether days in this city were tracked in the same way as outside. He confirmed that yes, the weeks here were the same, except without Mass, which made me happy because although I believe in God in my own way, I never understood why we had to repeat the same thing every week at the same time and in the same place when He supposedly told us He was everywhere all the time. After agreeing to Sunday and confirming it again, we hugged each other goodbye with one of those long hugs men give each other when they're drunk, and then each of us went off to try to find his own home, or at least that's what I did.

I lost sight of the former agent as he turned a corner, and I headed in the other direction, more to avoid following him than because I knew where I was going. If before the city had been easy for me to navigate, now, between the distraction and the beer, I couldn't figure out where I was. Everything was so identical that I wondered how anyone found their way, and I must have taken a hundred turns before seeing my wife through the walls, sitting on her bed with a look on her face that said, now you'll see what's what. The sight of her was frightening and comforting at the same time. Frightening because of what was in store for me, and comforting because I'd finally and by my own wits found my home.

In the glass elevator I tried to fix myself up, and before I opened the glass door I smoothed my hair the way you do when you're trying to comb it hastily and too late, though I could see her and I knew that in this transparent world there was no way of hiding anything, not even for an instant, that it wasn't necessary to open a door to see how bad I looked.

Since the boy was already asleep, there was no shouting, nor did she ask for explanations. She only said that she'd been horribly worried about me, that it was better to go straight to bed, that it was late and we weren't going to get enough rest before work tomorrow. I splashed my face in the transparent bathroom, a short distance from a man, my neighbor, who seemed to be doing his business, with little success, and then, queasy from all of this and not having eaten dinner, I went to bed.

As always happens, my night of partying wasn't worth the trouble it brought me, and as I fell asleep I swore not to do it again, no matter how much cold beer they gave away in this city without walls or however I might long to remember, from time to time, the way things were in the life before this one.

If I didn't kiss her that night, it was to spare her my breath, and not because I didn't love her, and also because I was still used to that other life and forgot for a moment that nothing smelled here. I suppose fear takes longer to remove than odor, perhaps forever.

◈

In the morning I was running late because of my hangover, and she and the boy left home before me. Also, why deny it, I straggled to avoid seeing them, or to avoid them seeing me. When I got to work, I was almost glad to hop on the tractor and drag my little train of excrement without anyone caring whether I'd gone out and for how long or whether I'd had this or that to drink the night before. Sometimes a job, however crude it might be, is the best comfort for a man who doesn't want to talk to anyone or give too many explanations. At mealtime I was in higher spirits, and since you could choose to eat at the long table in the dining hall or take your tray into the garden, I went outside so I could at least look at the trees and take a break from the white basement, which, though it was as transparent as everything else in this city, was much farther down and the sight of so many people above could sometimes weigh on you. There were plants in the garden, and a fountain and small trees, and when you looked up you could see the dome, which was so high and luminous that it looked a great deal like a white and cloudless sky. One of those skies that threatens snow, but without the cold, of course.

At the snack break I was almost fully recovered and was plotting how to get back to the bar, if I could find it again, to drink just one beer, maybe two, to gather my courage before heading home.

I found the bar more easily than I thought I would, and although at first I was disappointed not to see the former zone agent, who you could say was my only friend, later I was glad he wasn't there, as this allowed me to fulfill my promise, and after my second beer I went right home like a good boy.

She, who loved me, didn't say a word about the night before, and the three of us had dinner together, if not cheerfully, at least in peace. As usual, the kid didn't make a peep, but she told me he'd come home from school with a note of praise for his excellent behavior and that he'd sat down to his homework and gotten it all done, which pleased me. My sons had been good students too, and I'm not the kind of man to put up with laziness under his roof.

I went right to bed without looking at the animal encyclopedia, and she and Julio stayed up a good while reading real books, and I even thought I heard, through half-sleep, her voice telling him a story before putting the eye mask on the kid and coming to bed by my side. That night we didn't kiss either, but this time it was because she didn't want to. And when I tried to get something going beneath the sheets, she made it clear there would be none of that, which seemed odd, since in our other life she'd always been very fiery.

I don't know if it was because she'd denied me her affections or because of everything that had happened since I burned the house or even before that, when the boys were no longer home and the land bore no fruit, or when we let them take our chickens and horses, but I was noticing something strange between us, in the us that was once just ours, and I thought about it so much that who knows how long I lay there wearing that eye mask without a wink of sleep. As for her, I could hear her breathing deeply, as she always did when she slept, in a way that's not the same as snoring. I was a snorer, a heavy one at that, to the point where I'd wake myself up with my own noises. Normally her breathing calmed me, and if for whatever reason, because of normal day-to-day worries, I had a hard time going to sleep, it was enough to hear her and align my breath with hers and I'd fall asleep, but now, here, in this city without night and in this bed we hadn't bought or chosen and with this stolen or borrowed kid in the room and in this crystal life, I found it impossible to sleep, and the more I tried, the more clearly I saw that there was no way, so in the end I gave up and got up very carefully so I wouldn't wake her. I took off the eye mask and looked around the room in a night without moon or darkness or anything at all, and I saw all those sleeping people, thousands and thousands of strangers sleeping so peacefully, and it all seemed like a horrific nightmare I couldn't wake up from except by falling asleep and, in my dreams, returning to the forest to find the place outside where, in reality, in the reality we had before, I'd buried my shotguns.

That's how I spent the hours, sitting on the bed, not

knowing what to do, turning the most frightening thoughts around and around in my head and wanting desperately to get out of this city even though they took care of us so thoroughly and so well. As always happens with insomnia, at some point I must have fallen asleep without knowing exactly when. Because suddenly she was waking me, and this time there was a kiss as well as breakfast already prepared and on the table.

Since I hadn't slept well, that morning I did everything slowly, with that feeling you get when you haven't rested, like walking in mud with leaden feet. I barely arrived at work on time, and no matter how much coffee I drank I couldn't rouse myself completely, nor did I speak to anyone, nor was I in a good mood, and after the snack break, when the workday was almost done, the thing I'd been fearing all day happened: I got distracted, accelerated the tractor too soon, and rear-ended the tractor in front of me. The collision was dramatic, considering how slowly we'd been going. I fell to the ground and made the other driver fall too and the odorless shit scattered everywhere and I got a reprimand and was taken right to the supervisor and, from there, to the doctor's office.

The doctor was concerned about my insomnia and my miserable appearance, and he said it was normal to experience stress in times of change and adjustment, and maybe what I needed was a counselor. I asked whether he meant a shrink, and he assured me that no, there were none of

those in this city, that psychology in general wasn't held
in very high regard, and he told me that certain mild nervous disorders like the one that was surely afflicting me
now were left in the hands of counselors, people who
were trained to listen with empathy, and that this was often more than enough and worked better than any pills
or torturous sessions of psychoanalysis. I asked whether a
counselor like that wasn't really a priest, and he laughed
and said no, there weren't any priests in the city either, nor
were they missed. Finally, I wanted to know whether the
counseling was mandatory, a kind of punishment for having crashed my tractor. Again the good doctor made light
of my concern and made it clear that this was not a punishment at all, it was just an option and it was up to me, and
in any case he'd give me a pill that would help me rest immediately and a note excusing me from work for two days
so I could fully recuperate.

❖

I left the doctor's office and went to change. My coworkers
cheered me up, and the supervisor patted me on the back
reassuringly as if to put it all behind us. They all wished
me a smooth recovery and a swift return. To tell you the
truth, they made me feel better, I don't like to miss work,

I've never liked to, nor am I one to get sick for no reason, and I generally see myself as a strong man who doesn't shirk his responsibilities. Back on the land, even before it was mine, nobody ever saw me falter on the job, nor did any coughs or fevers keep me from my labors, and if we had to get up when even the rooster was still asleep, I was the first one there, and if we had to haul wheat to the silo by moonlight, nobody saw me so much as yawn. When it came to doing what had to be done, no laborer worked harder than me, and when it came to overseeing the land and the house's provisions, never had a more rigorous and devoted foreman ever been born. If now — at this incredibly simple job of hauling shit back and forth, which obviously was not harder or more demanding than the tasks I was used to — I faltered, it couldn't be blamed on my condition or, obviously, on my constitution, but rather on something that even I couldn't pinpoint and that would never have happened to me in the world I used to know. In other words, I was and always have been an upright man, a hard worker who'd takes his duties seriously and who'd carry whatever needed carrying on his back like a donkey without complaint, with sweat on his forehead and honest dreams. I'd dragged not a thousand sacks of grain but many more than that, in my other life, without so much as making a face, and dragging shit with a tractor was neither below me nor too much for me. So this new me who went off the rails and went home ill at the end of the workday wasn't like me, and I didn't recognize him, nor did I like him. No weight was easy for me to carry, not potatoes, not wheat, not wood, not flour, but I did it. Being unable to finish a task, no matter what it was, made me feel indebted to the entire world, and, above all, indebted to however little of me there was.

❖

I went home with the pills to help me rest and with the formal doctor's note. The apartment was empty and so were the ones around it, so for once I could sit there without seeing all those people with whom I felt forced to share my privacy day and night. I took my pill and lay down in bed, and before long I fell into a deep sleep.

I WOKE UP TWO DAYS LATER. SHE WAS PREPARING BREAK-
fast and Julio was still asleep. She asked me how I felt,
and I said dazed, and that's when she told me how long
I'd slept, and it scared me. I couldn't believe I'd really
slept more than forty-eight hours in a row. When I stood
up, I was dizzy, and she tenderly helped me to the table.
Then she woke the kid and we all had breakfast together,
and thanks to the orange juice and cereal and two eggs,
I started feeling better. I was ravenous, but she wouldn't

let me stuff myself because it wasn't good for me, and she was right. After breakfast I took a shower. On the other side of the glass wall the same neighbor showered every morning, but we never waved hello or anything like it, what's more, we acted as if we couldn't see each other, and the truth is that with so much seeing people, in the end it's as if they don't exist, and I suppose I had the same effect on others, too. In any case, in the shower I started feeling stronger and in better spirits, almost happy, and I sang an old song to myself, a song from school that suddenly sprang to mind, though I don't know why. I'd woken up in a state of confusion, but when I emerged from the shower and got dressed I noticed that my head was working marvelously again and that made me feel good, able and ready for anything. I was eager to get to work and show them all that I'd fully recovered and that I could be counted on and the accident with the tractor wouldn't happen again and that I planned not to go off the rails anymore and that the shit they put me in charge of each day was in good hands.

I was in such a good mood when I left home that I felt things couldn't go too badly, and indeed, I had my best day yet. I carried out my work impeccably, and contrary to the days preceding the accident, I didn't find my task boring or insignificant. Everything in this life must be done with attention and care, and hauling a worm of excrement is no exception. I'd already seen what could happen the minute you get sloppy and don't keep all your senses alert. I'd learned my lesson. The bottom line is that people who complain about the work bestowed on them by fate, instead of thanking God, they harbor an unwholesome arrogance and think they deserve better, and that's how it goes in life. The dissatisfied always think they deserve more than they've been given, and their complaining turns them into weak, useless people. The kind that ask the earth to bear fruit without putting in any effort.

I wasn't the sort of man to go around crying or cursing my fortune, and I didn't know what had come over me during those days I spent poisoning myself with twisted thoughts and baseless anxiety. Now that I'd recovered, I felt I was myself again, but a better version of myself, calmer and more centered, more prepared to fulfill my duties flawlessly and without protest and, why not say it, be more excited about what the present had to offer. The past and the future started to release me from the sinister shadows of nostalgia and ambition, which are like grasping hands that can drown a man, and I could clearly see that by doing what I'd been ordered to do and doing it well, with great care, I'd have more than enough to be content. I thanked God that I had a job, a woman like her by my side, a place to live, and a boy like Julio, who was healthy and happy, to keep us company, and I only asked the Lord

for Augusto and Pablo — whether they were dead or alive
— to have in that same instant the same spiritual peace
that I enjoyed.

❖

During lunch, my coworkers were very thoughtful; they
asked me about my brief illness with genuine concern and
they were glad to see me so fully recovered and in a better state than before. We joked around good-naturedly
and talked about the things men talk about when they eat:
family, women, and even hunting, as among my coworkers there were at least two fellow enthusiasts. The whole
day was so pleasant that it went by fast, and when I was in
the shower I almost felt sad to be going back home, though
once I hit the streets I went directly there, whistling and eager to embrace her when I arrived and thank her for all the
things she did for me, and wanting also to see the boy and
ask about his progress at school. I realized that since we arrived I hadn't given Julio enough attention, and I missed
playing with him and hearing him laugh, so I decided to
change this. Naturally, it didn't cross my mind to stop at
the bar, and I couldn't understand why the hell I'd gone
there or what sorrows I'd been trying to drown in beer,
since I didn't have any sorrows, not real ones.

It's remarkable how, when you find yourself in such a good state, ideas arrive clearly in your mind, no cliffs, no labyrinths, and how feelings settle gently in your chest and find a home there, strong and beautiful, as fear disappears. Basically, I was doing better than great, in fact I was so well, so happy, so loving, that I started wondering what the hell kind of pill that doctor had given me. I kept walking down the street full of a happiness so intense that it had me soaring, and I couldn't do anything to stop it. A happiness so intense, so broad, and so unfounded that, to tell you the truth, it was starting to crush me.

WHEN I GOT HOME, SHE HAD A SMALL SURPRISE FOR ME: we had company over for dinner. In fact, it was only one person, that handsome young man I'd seen at the public library when I accompanied her there on the second day. I didn't have to open the door to see him, as from the elevator I saw the two of them, the good-looking guy and her, setting the table and joking around and having a fine old time. I couldn't hear them yet, but I could tell they were getting along famously and had established quite the rapport at work. Upon seeing them, I tried to sour my mood, but I couldn't. Instead of the feeling I was after, I found another one, inappropriate generosity, and I became happy to my core, without being able to prevent it, to see her so delighted by the company of another man. When I entered the apartment and she introduced him to me, although I'd already seen him and had my eye on him, I couldn't look at him mistrustfully, as I had intended, but rather gave him my biggest and most honest smile and a sincere hug. I told him to make himself at home, though I hoped he wouldn't forget that he was in mine.

I embraced Julio, and sat down on the floor to play with him and praised him effusively, enjoying my child like an idiot while she and her friend went on preparing dinner, and he became more entranced with her with every passing minute. And, I hate to say it, she with him as well. Not only did each laugh at everything the other one said, as if it were the funniest thing in the world, they also found excuses to brush up against each other. They weren't frotting in front of me, no, but they went out of their way to find the slightest reason to pat each other on the shoulder, make a gesture, stand too close while opening the escarole for the salad — you know, the kinds of things that on their own don't mean very much but when taken together speak to open collusion. I was startled that in so little time they'd become so close, so connected, so . . . whatever it was. I wanted to find, inside myself, the energy to stop that

man in his tracks, but instead I shocked myself by opening
the bottle of wine he'd brought in our honor and pouring
it out, for him, for her, and a little for me, and I sat down
at the table and listened with utterly rapt attention while
the young guy talked. And little by little, to my dismay,
he started to seem intelligent, educated, and completely
charming. And don't let me forget to mention his way
with children. Julio stayed by his side throughout dinner,
and when we finished he showed the man his schoolwork
and drawings, and with all the compliments the polite visi-
tor gave the kid, Julio got excited and even drew the man's
portrait in charcoal, in great detail, achieving an astonishing likeness. The truth is, the boy was a real artist. Julio
gave him the picture as a present, and if only he'd taken it
home, but no, she had to tape it to the door of the fridge,
and there it stayed. Later I was fool enough to take the boy
aside and, sitting on my bed, we started reading our animal
encyclopedia while the young man and my wife sat on the
sofa and discussed books and a thousand other important
things with all the culture they had and I did not.

I was the one to tuck the kid into bed while the handsome and brilliant young man said good night. Then I went
to give him another hug, more sincere than the first one, if
that's possible, and the worst thing of all is that as he was finally walking out, I stood there staring at him, spellbound.
I couldn't help feeling a little sad, as he was such a nice guy
that his mere presence lit up the home and made you feel

good and at ease, even though he'd been flirting all night
—or so it seemed to me—with my wife, and tricking her
into only having eyes and ears for him. So I couldn't stop
myself from missing him already as we watched him descend in the elevator and wave his hand in a warm goodbye, a gesture I returned with a wave of my own hand
without wanting to do it. I surprised myself by asking her
when our guest would return and remarking that a young
man as fantastic as he deserved our deepest friendship, and
adding how happy I was that she'd found such a polite and
interesting coworker with whom to share the long days at
the library. Why I behaved the way I did, why I said what I
said, and, above all, how I could have felt what I felt is all a
mystery to me, and the worst part is, having betrayed my
own habits and my own nature so completely, I must admit that I'd never felt better in my life, nor more comfortable with my feelings or more in alignment with the uni-
verse.

What's certain is that ever since they made me burn my
house and pack our suitcases, I'd tried hard to adapt to
whatever became of my life, but I'd never dreamed that I
would end up like this, that I could be so happy in the middle of misfortune, and that I could feel this way against my
own will.

THE NEXT DAY, I RUSHED TO THE DOCTOR'S OFFICE DUR-ing our lunch break. The doctor, as was to be expected, denied having given me any strange drugs and told me that what I felt was nothing more than the fruits of a perfect final adjustment to my new life, and that I should be celebrating instead of asking myself unsettling questions that would achieve nothing but a return of anxiety, boredom, and insomnia. I replied that there was no need for him to worry about that one bit because, as a matter of fact, I spent the whole day internally celebrating everything, to the point where I no longer knew what I was celebrating, but far from getting angry or disturbed, I celebrated my uncertainty and ignorance, and the truth was that I could not for a single second stop celebrating everything and I was even celebrating this very conversation I was having with him, but not as much as I would surely celebrate leaving his office to return to work.

He asked whether I'd had lunch, and I replied that I had not, but this also made me glad, because now I'd enjoy my afternoon snack break all the more. And then, indeed, I left the doctor's office and returned to work in a happy state.

There was something about the city and all its affairs that made you unable to complain about a thing, not because they didn't let you talk — they did — but rather because you couldn't muster a complaint about how well everything worked, and in the depths of your soul you had nothing but a sense of contentment that never left you, and as there was nothing significant to fear or hope for about tomorrow, it wasn't easy to feel anxious either, or scared in that vague way I used to feel back on my land because of the war, or the safety of my loved ones, or the wolves that prowled around the chicken coops by night. It's odd to realize that negative emotions can be missed, and that without fear of any kind you sleep great but wake

up in a strange state. After so many nights of going to bed
without fear, I'd started seeming like a different person to
myself, one who couldn't quite be trusted. The transparent city had no churches, so if you wanted to confess anything, you had to confess to yourself. And as I said, I didn't
dare confess how fed up I was and how much it was weigh-
ing me down to be happy all the time without knowing
why. There was also the option of talking to one of the
counselors from the union, but I have to admit that since
entering the city I was wary of trusting others enough to
open up about what was going on inside me, and it's possible that the same was true before I arrived. I've never
been one to go crying to people about my problems, because my guess is that everyone's got plenty to deal with
on their own, and what's more, nobody really cares what
happens to people other than themselves. People act as if
they care a great deal about others, but I don't buy it, not
about people here or anywhere else. Nor do I believe that
priests give a rat's ass, to be frank, nor does it seem possible
that God knows all of us by name. In short, when it comes
to what a man carries in his heart or mind, there's no one
who cares about it beyond the man himself, and that's
why from a very young age I decided not to go around telling people my business. Now that I was no longer capable
of recognizing my own doubts, or understanding whether
I truly felt this way or that, I was as alone as a stranded

man, and more silenced than my little Julio, since I figured he must at least talk to himself with the clear voice of his soul, something that I'd stopped doing without even being aware of it. As if we were two people walking side by side without saying a word.

◆◆◆

The days went by without incident. My perennial happiness stuck to me the way goat poop sticks to your hunting boots. And as if that weren't enough bad news, the handsome young man from the library came to visit us more often. Twice a week at first, but soon almost every night. He showed great interest not only in her, but also in the kid, with whom he read books and played I don't know what math games. They surely didn't read the animal encyclopedia, as I hid it every time the interloper came. I'm far from well read, but I do know a thing or two, and it seemed to me that the handsome young man from the library read the kid such complicated things that he couldn't possibly understand them. But Julio clearly got excited and drew endless pictures that the handsome young man stared at in admiration. She was happy, and given my state of perpetual enchantment, so was I; nothing that took place in my life, no matter how weird or un-

settling, could sadden me. You could even say that I found
a certain harmony in the presence of that young man who
showered us with attention, and I gladly drank his wine,
he usually brought a bottle of red, and sometimes I was
the first to go to sleep. I liked dozing off to the sound of
them talking about wise, important things that didn't
concern me at all.

⬦

As I said, this new routine didn't disgust me at first, nor
did it manage to bother me as time passed. I even bragged
at work about how smart he was, this young librarian
who came to our house all the time, and the oddest part is
that none of my coworkers at the recycling center seemed
to find my situation unusual, nor did anyone make any
biting comments, so I started thinking that what was happening to me—whatever these absurd attacks of happiness were that caused me to accept everything as if it were
normal, this vague and forced well-being that had turned
me into a moron—had also happened to them a long
time ago.

I couldn't believe that in this new world, in this transparent city, nothing mattered. That a handsome young
man hovering around your wife, in your own home, was

the same as a union vote to call for more oil for the tractors' connecting rods. Granted, the tractors squeaked,
but still, didn't these good people have anything better to think about? There was so much blind trust in this
city that in the end you couldn't help feeling uneasy, or at
least trying to feel uneasy, as actually feeling uneasy was
hard to do because of how contented you were about everything, and, what's more, without good reason. When
an issue presented itself, whether something at work or
at home, you couldn't put up any resistance, since in every detail you found, against your own will, a thousand
reasons to feel the deepest peace, and everything always
worked splendidly. And if you had to spend your day hauling shit around, you did it gladly, and if you had to put
up with nightly visits from a handsome young man who
hit on your wife while he made your little one's head spin,
well, you'd lick it all up and say you liked it, and that's how
things kept going without a single protest from you. The
city was perfect, and complaining about perfection is for
madmen, and in the absence of big problems, which we
didn't have here, only those with bad faith would raise
their voices, and since you couldn't find bad faith of your
own even by turning all your pockets inside out, there was
no choice but to shut up and swallow it. And I shut up and
I swallowed, day after day and night after night, aware —
this much was true — of the fact that I was betraying my

own nature, but also aware that I'm no idiot, that my nature was out of place in this city, and that even if I had the courage to look for my old nature, to use it the way you'd use a lever to budge a rock, I wouldn't be able to find it, and when I say *find it*, I don't know whether I'm referring to the lever, my nature, or the rock, as the more I swallowed, the more everything confused me. How can a man lose his own inner self and, along with it, everything that gives meaning to his small intellect? I couldn't say. That it can be lost in certain circumstances is the one thing I've come to know for sure.

One ordinary day, when I got home after work, something finally took place that was different, though I'm afraid to say it wasn't entirely surprising.

There he was, the handsome young man. But this time he was alone with her, as it seemed the kid had extracurricular activities from which he had not yet returned. I asked her what those activities were while, if I recall correctly, she finished buttoning up her blouse and gathering her hair into a hasty ponytail.

She looked at me without a trace of shame, with affection, as her friend put on his trousers in the transparent bedroom. I waited in silence as the young man got dressed. Then he emerged and explained, in great detail, every single one of Julio's extracurricular activities.

According to the librarian, the rigorous exams our beloved Julio had taken at school left no doubt and clearly marked the kid as special, and not just a little bit special but highly so, and as a result our good Julio had been included in a program that offered orientation, nutrition, and guidance for exceptional minds, destined to safeguard and motivate his abilities. It goes without saying that this made me very happy, yet I wanted to ask him what that had to do with his screwing my wife in my own home. I say *wanted to ask,* not that I did so, because the good man would not stop singing Julio's praises and citing scientific facts about those damn tests he'd been given and how, according to him, I didn't understand them, but they clearly showed this was a truly unique case of a boy whose special abilities transcended the average of the normally special child. I was wondering what that average might be and what those other normally special children might be like when the young man put an end to my doubts by confessing that he himself had been a highly special child, though not as special as our kid, and that where he'd been seen as a highly special specimen, Julio was doubly so in any and all areas of specialness. Which I was glad about, because at least someone in my home, though it wasn't me, could doubly beat that adorable librarian at something.

The young man, however, corrected my first impression by warning that the manner in which the boy was special and the manner in which he himself was special were in fact quite different, and that actually, if you had to put it into words, you could call them opposite ways of being exceptional.

All this coded language had me tangled up, and I felt obliged to ask whether the kid was, in fact, very sharp or very dumb. The young man scolded me severely, saying that this was far from the appropriate question and that this was precisely the kind of thing that made the world such an unjust place for special beings. Since I did not want to be unjust toward special beings or toward any other kind of being and I had no questions aside from that one, I shut up.

Later she explained to me that, given Julio's exceptional circumstances, the education committee had decided that the kid would need not only a tailored training program different from the schooling of other kids his age, but also a personal supervisor, a tutor who'd stay by his side as a supplementary aide in the years to come. And to be honest, I wasn't remotely surprised to learn who had been chosen to carry out such an important task. None other than our young and well-equipped friend, who'd been generous enough to request a transfer from the public library in or-der to personally take responsibility day and night — and apparently in the midafternoon as well — not only for Ju-lio's well-being, but for that of our entire family.

I was so delighted by this good news that I was on the verge of doing cartwheels, and I had to shut myself in the bathroom, where I tried to calm my euphoria and search my soul for some shred of my old self, but it was useless, I couldn't find it, and what my wife and that so-called active supervisor of my new family life saw through the walls as I tried unsuccessfully to cry was the same thing I saw, to my dismay, in the mirror: the face of a man absurdly satisfied with his fate.

❖

That night, when Julio finally arrived home from his extra-curricular activities, we celebrated the good news together as a family, that is to say, she, I, the kid, and, obviously, the young former librarian who was now a tutor, and then we all — and when I say *all*, I mean him, too — went to bed.

Well, actually, not me. From that night on, I slept on the sofa.

While she and the handsome young usurper got into what until yesterday had been my bed, Julio and I looked over our old animal encyclopedia. The kid's face lit up at the sight of the strangest beasts, and he cracked up at the duck-billed platypus.

   In truth, I don't know exactly how special he was, but to me he seemed witty as hell.

THE FOLLOWING DAYS WENT BY WITHOUT A STIR. WORK went well, there were no mishaps, accidents, or conflicts. My supervisor recommended me for a promotion that never seemed to come. I didn't care. Promotions were voted on in the union and they always seemed to vote for someone else; to be honest, I didn't vote for my own promotion because I didn't want to be promoted. I was fine the way I was, I'd gotten used to doing my duty without complaint and happily, of course, as there was no other way.

I took part in endless votes on other matters: on our section representative, on the chief of command, on something or other related to the cleaning service. Every two or three weeks there was a vote about something, so much voting that you ended up losing interest. On the other hand, everything in the city worked, basic necessities were well handled, and I couldn't think of any better way to run things. All of this made me more apathetic when it came time to vote.

❖

Julio's young and handsome tutor adapted smoothly to the new arrangement. So did she. Only once did it occur to me to ask her whether she missed me. She said no, because when it came down to it she still had me close by; she also said that these things happen to couples and there was no need to give it much importance. Lastly, she said that I'd changed a great deal, that I wasn't even the shadow of the man I'd been. I thanked her for her frankness.

Since I had plenty of free time and little to do at home after work, I signed up for a brief course on personal growth. There I was taught to express myself properly and organize my priorities. The class was free, as was everything in our damn city, but you learned a great deal very rapidly. Once I'd learned how to organize my priorities I realized that I had no priorities to organize, but my teacher told me not to worry, that the course would still come in handy for organizing other things—my sock drawer, for example. Nothing could have been truer, my four pairs of socks were perfectly organized from then on. When I grew tired of organizing and admiring the way things looked in their organized state, I signed up for a ping-pong tournament through the union. It went swimmingly. My self-esteem rose. My trainer told me that if I got serious they might put me on the national championship team representing the union of excrement drivers. I asked him where that championship took place, and he said, all over the country. The idea sounded marvelous to me, because I still didn't really know what country I lived in, or how the other one out there had ended up, and this would give me the chance to see a thing or two. I was excited to see the countryside, or what remained of it, and maybe—since I was already dreaming big—I could even visit my old region. I started training like a man possessed, and one after the other I beat all my coworkers fair and square, and, of course, my popularity took a downturn. Barely anyone spoke to me in the dining hall. Some people are sore losers. Over time, I started letting my coworkers win a little, to see whether they'd stop ghosting me, but it was too late, because some people not only are sore losers but never let go of a grudge. In any case, the whole ping-pong thing didn't do me any good, and it infuriated me, because I think I had a natural talent for it. All that letting other people win made my scores drop without getting me back into my peers' good graces. I saw clearly that the ill will my victories had inspired would not be erased by my humiliation. The union's national championship was held without me, and someone else won. Still, I kept playing every afternoon, because, whether I won or let others win, it kept me entertained.

I wasn't the only one who made extraordinary progress during that time, though in my case it didn't get me far. Julio started at his special school and blew all his teachers away. They gave him so many certificates of achievement that we didn't know where to put them. He was growing up healthy, happy, and strong. He was still very affectionate with me, and although he spent most of his time in class or with the young tutor who lived in our home and slept with my wife, he still knew I was his father. Or, at least, the closest thing he had to a father. Sometimes he came to see me at ping-pong games, and he clapped like crazy even when I lost on purpose, maybe because he didn't know.

We were proud of each other.

My tremendous happiness was gradually seeming more and more natural, though it was nothing of the kind. Or, at least, my inability to get upset was starting to feel less strange.

I was becoming tired, I suppose, like an old dog, accepting that things are as they are and will continue that way until something or someone changes them. And, why deny it, I knew I was not that person. Just as old dogs lie down and accept their circumstances, I too lay down, half asleep, complying with the invisible orders of fate.

Once you admit that God hasn't chosen you to do anything extraordinary, you start to really live the way you should, with your hands and feet inside a circle marked in the sand, not stepping out beyond your terrain or hankering for what isn't yours.

My unjustified happiness and I were making peace with each other, as I mentioned, so that I barely noticed anymore that I was constantly happier than I should be.

At night I slept serenely. I went to bed on the sofa, across from Julio's bed, and we looked at each other before putting our eye masks on and surrendering to sleep. I'd say good night and he'd smile and say nothing. He still didn't talk, but the doctors assured us that there was nothing wrong with his vocal cords, that he simply preferred to be silent. It seemed odd to me that anyone would truly prefer never to speak, but I'm no doctor and the kid seemed to be doing fine. She, on the other hand, didn't seem very happy, I suppose she did what she did and slept with the young tutor because she thought it the best thing for Julio. We didn't speak to each other much, she and I, as she was almost always with the handsome young man, who no longer struck me as so young or so handsome, and who, of this I was sure, had begun to go bald.

For my part, I had a few flings, two to be exact, with women from the relief services, the kind who used to be called whores, but not here and rightly so, as they didn't charge for helping you out and were very warm and polite. If I didn't go more often, it was because I couldn't adjust to fucking in full view of everyone in one of those transparent brothels, and also because she received a report every time. For some reason that escapes me, in the transparent city reports must be drawn up on everything you do, even though everything is completely visible and there's nowhere to hide.

I also had a flirtation with a coworker, but it never went very far; we groped each other a bit in the showers and that was it. The thing is, I can't really pull it off in the shower, people are watching and I lose what I have going. Others don't care, and in fact it's a rare day that you don't see a pair of coworkers putting on a show, but as I said, I can't get used to it. I suppose it's because I'm old-fashioned and the type to do it with the lights off, which, in this place, is clearly impossible.

✧

And that's something that exists in the transparent city
like no other place I've known: visibility. You can have a
good or bad opinion about visibility, but when it's as ex-
cessive as this and becomes the only available condition,
it devours all secrets, all mysteries, and all desire. And so
much of seeing everything makes you lose your impulse
to pay attention to anything. I remember that in the countryside, during the harvest, we'd look for shade without
giving it much thought, as the natural thing to do. Nature
had its nooks and shadows, and it seems to me that the architects who built this city could learn a thing or two from
it. Those architects who built this crystal city, so perpetu-
ally full of light, so clear, so perfect.

✧

Sometimes, back on our land, the sun bore down and made
it unbearable to be outside or inside. We'd open the windows at night and drink lemonade, but nothing eased our
sweat or discomfort, and as the seasons turned we lived a
very different life, a world naturally becoming its own op-

posite. During the harsh winters, we took refuge under blankets, dined near the hearth, and wrapped our hands in rags to keep from getting chilblains. Rural life teaches you the limits of things, of strength and of people's character; it teaches you that the earth is in charge.

In that other life, nobody seemed to be in charge. In the life that I considered mine before, nothing seemed to control behavior, and yet people behaved decently and obeyed, even if they didn't know exactly what they were obeying. It could have been the red embers in your fire, or the bedbugs hiding in your wool mattress, or the grime under your fingernails. Cold and heat. And obeying nature, to my mind, organized things, or at least gave them an order of some kind. Red and black and white are more obeyed, and better obeyed, than all this transparency. You respond to things that are real, that are solid and offer cover, since whenever one thing is covered, another is revealed. But the clear sight of everything weighs down a person's spirits. Nobody wants to go hunting and discover that the animals, against their own better instincts, no longer hide. By the same token, I imagine nobody wants to be exposed all the time once he knows he's the prey. That's all to say that this life without storms or torments was beyond my understanding, nor did I have any desire to understand it.

Aside from that, I can't deny that in the transparent city we never wanted for anything and they even allowed us to exchange gifts at Christmas. One per person, taken from a list of useful items provided in advance: nail clippers, trivets, small cups for holding boiled eggs, an ointment for muscle pain (I was occasionally sore from playing ping-pong), things like that. All you had to do was mark a box with an X for the appointed person to receive the selected gift, so it wasn't anything out of this world, nor did it bring much joy, but they were still gifts when it came down to it and they made the holidays more cheerful. I received enough ointment for a lifetime, considering I had only a small injury on one elbow, but that's how everything went in the transparent city: they gave you a lot of what you didn't want, and none of what you really missed.

The only two holidays were Christmas and Victory Day. The truth is that Victory Day commemorated the day of defeat for all of us who lived inside, but nobody seemed to remember this, not even me. Large tables were placed on the street, and sausages and beer were given out; it was the closest thing to a popular festival in the city, and everyone had a blast, including me, or at least we all gave the appearance of being very happy. If you ask me, it should have been called Evacuation Day or Permanent Removal Day or End of Life As You Knew It Day, but nobody ever asked me, so I kept my opinions to myself.

❖

We didn't really make friends, at least I didn't, because she and that dandy of a tutor sometimes went to meetings for a kind of book club, where it seemed that they discussed what they'd been reading with other educated people like them. I wasn't invited, but if I had been, I wouldn't have wanted to go. I've never had much use for books unless they include pictures of animals or nature, and I don't understand why so much importance is given to stories that are all made up and thin on truth. My guess is that people who are short on courage enjoy fantasy, and that men who are as manly as God intended prefer what we can see and touch, but to each his own.

As for my coworkers, I've already said that the more I excelled at ping-pong, the worse they treated me, and my trainer, who at first held me in high esteem, turned his back on me when I started letting others win. So in the end I was alone, between one rejection and the other. For entertainment, I went to the movies once in a while, but the movies were old and almost always musicals, which make me a little nervous, as I also can't understand how people could spend their days dancing and singing when what's normal is to walk and talk. Once or twice I tried to remark on this, but there was always someone in the audience who shushed me, which I can understand. If you're enjoying a movie, it's annoying for someone else to spoil it, and when it came down to it, the fact that musicals bored me was nobody else's fault.

Going to the movies was just a way of killing time and avoiding my home, since, though no one said this aloud, I felt unnecessary there, though that feeling didn't rub me the wrong way or sadden me, nor did I give a damn. I did feel good around the kid, and it seemed that he felt the same way about me, but with him being mute and me not being much of a conversationalist I can't say we did much chatting. We laughed a lot, it's true, but I'm not sure about what. We kept each other company like a boy and his dog, who can be best friends without exchanging a word. Nothing else really mattered to me.

I think that, without realizing it, I'd been losing interest in almost everything. I couldn't care less about politics, local or international, and not even at work could I care much about the union's intrigues, because despite the fact that they asked our opinion and took votes on every little matter, they seemed perfectly organized without any help from me and I didn't have the ability or intelligence —much less the urge—to try to improve on what anyone was doing.

Sometimes I took long strolls, not going very far, but tracing long circles through the crowds, watching other people's lives through walls without finding them to be very different from mine, without envying anyone or harboring any resentments. Only occasionally, at the sight of a particularly affectionate or passionate couple, did I miss what she and I had had before we were torn from our land. I also recall that, on hearing a man shout wildly on the street during one of my walks, I longed for a second to be that man, though he was clearly deranged. The poor guy was hollering into the crowd without anyone paying him the slightest attention, completely enraged, and I suppose it was his anger that I longed to find inside myself, that I suddenly missed.

A long time went by almost without my realizing it, and I would have gone a lot longer without anything worth telling if it hadn't been for one afternoon when, I couldn't tell you why, I decided to skip ping-pong and, instead of going to the sports center for my daily practice session, I found myself walking toward the old bar. I hadn't had a beer in ages, nor had I missed it, but that day my thirst was back. They say you can easily take a man out of his home, but it's much harder to take the home out of the man. They may be right.

It took me a while to find the bar, in this city everything looks so similar that you immediately forget how you got somewhere, but after a few false turns through those identical streets, I came upon it. There it was, as transparent and lively as always. I found a spot at the bar and asked for a nice cold one. I was enjoying my first sip — there's nothing in this world or the next one like that first sip of ice-cold beer — when someone touched my shoulder. I turned, and who was standing there? My friend, my only friend, the former zone agent. What a hug we gave each other! It goes without saying that he sat down next to me and ordered another beer. We started chatting like old pals, though we'd never been such a thing. Neither his life nor mine had much to show for the lapsed time, but it didn't matter. The forced bond of people from the same region kept the conversation going. He was enormously happy to hear all the good things that had happened to me — the ping-pong, the special kid who kept getting certificates as rewards for his singularity. He didn't have children, and people without kids often see them as possessing magical qualities, as if they couldn't possibly grow up to become like us, so he couldn't stop repeating that children are a treasure and a good fortune and a gift from the Lord and the salt of our lives. When I asked him about his life, I realized how little I knew about him. For one thing, I didn't know what he did for a living before becoming a zone agent during the war, nor, of course, what he

did for a living now. He told me that before the war he'd
been a thermostat technician at a foundry, but there was
no use for those skills here, since there was no heavy in-
dustrial work in the transparent city, so the first year he'd
been assigned to work as a glass cleaner, for which there
was plenty of need, and after the first year he was given a
management position at the arrival camp in return for his
good service as an agent during his region's evacuation. I
had no idea that the arrival camp was still in operation,
I'd thought that we'd all arrived long ago, but he told me
that it wasn't so, on the contrary, every day at least one
or two stragglers showed up. These stragglers were the
few who in some way or other had escaped the evacuation. Sometimes they were old people who'd disregarded
orders, or, more often, members of the defeated army.
Soldiers who'd sought refuge in the mountains or desert
caves so they wouldn't have to turn over their weapons. It
wasn't an organized resistance, but rather small, rebellious
clusters that were being eradicated little by little. Every
once in a while there were those who were unarmed and
had no bad intentions, who simply preferred not to live
in the transparent city. Suddenly I thought of my sons,
Augusto and Pablo, and wondered why I hadn't thought
of them more often, or every second of every day, and I
wanted to know whether they might have come to the arrival camp. The former zone agent told me that since he'd

been assigned there, they'd received more than two hundred stragglers, so it was impossible for him to know from just a first name, and, what's more, the information was confidential. I asked whether a father could try to find his own children, and he told me that it wasn't common but he could inquire, though he didn't seem too hopeful. We left the matter there and agreed to see each other again, and I reminded him that he still owed me a visit, as I'd invited him for Sunday dinner a long time ago and he'd never come. He apologized, saying he'd been very distracted, but then he confessed that soon after he saw me he'd met a good-looking woman and the whole thing slipped his mind. I then asked him about the woman in question, and he replied that it didn't work out, that she went off with another man. I followed one confession with another, saying that my love life wasn't exactly at its best either, and I told him about the imbecile who lived in my house and slept with my wife. He told me that this was normal here, and he brought up the joke about the horse who turned out to be a lawyer and the poor man who found him in bed with his wife when he arrived home from work. I didn't remember the ending of the joke, but since he was now laughing his head off as he recalled it, I laughed along, and soon we were both in stitches without knowing why, and the more we laughed, the more beer we ordered, and vice versa. So when we headed out

to the street we were pretty damn drunk and we parted
ways with an embrace and a promise to meet up again the
following day, same time. After all that, I still didn't know
the ending of the joke.

◈

Since not much happened during my days, the next morning at work I had trouble concentrating, caught up as
I was in my excitement about returning to the bar with
my friend and thinking he might bring some information
about my sons. It's not that anyone could tell, as by now
I did my work with my eyes closed, literally, but I felt different inside. It wasn't happiness, as this, unfortunately,
was my feeling all the time, but rather, finally, interest in
something, which was unusual. To do things right this
time, at the end of the workday I stopped in at the sports
center and falsely claimed I had an injury, and the trainer,
who I don't think really cared about this whole ping-pong
business, let me go without asking any questions. I went to
the bar and sat down with a beer, to wait. And I waited and
waited, but the former agent didn't show up. I wondered
whether it was possible that every time I made a plan with
this man he actually forgot or got swept up in a love af-

fair. It didn't seem likely. I then wondered whether the former zone agent could be avoiding me on purpose, but this didn't fit with the enthusiasm he'd shown during both our encounters. When the time arrived at which I'd be missed at home, I left. It's not that I was too concerned about her scolding me, since when it came down to it she was sleeping with another man right before my eyes, but I couldn't bear the idea of having to explain myself to that damn tutor. Ever since he'd moved in, he put a lot of effort into protecting us and acting as if he were ultimately responsible for all our lives. Yet I couldn't understand what she saw in him, beyond his gorgeous appearance and dazzling intellect.

I fell asleep worried that night, thinking of Augusto and Pablo more than I had in recent years, and I rebuked myself for not having done so more often, and for not having tried to look for them. It seemed inexplicable to me all of a sudden that she, their mother, hadn't urged me to do so, that she herself hadn't sought information about her sons. I didn't understand how we'd gone all this time without talking about our own children, or how we'd been able to forget them so — at least in my case — happily. Nor could I comprehend why I was always so glad about everything and why I couldn't muster a single complaint. For a long time now I'd wanted to worry about that, but I hadn't been able to. I concluded that this transparent city had done something odd to me and to my thoughts, and I deduced that, given that nobody had forced me to think this way or that, it all must be related to the water, since as soon as we arrived they made us undergo those crystallizations to avoid who knows what bacteria, and from that moment on I hadn't been the same, and every time I showered, I emerged less worried, and happier.

That very night I decided to stop showering.

Since I didn't want people to see that I wasn't showering, I decided not to change my alarm clock, which I didn't need anyway. It was enough to simply focus, before going to sleep, on the goal of waking up half an hour earlier. Back when I tilled the land and hunted and had a real life, I never needed an alarm clock, nor did I need dawn or a rooster's crowing to get me up. It was enough to decide it. Nor did I bathe every day before or during the war — much less twice a day as we did here, or even three times, as we also had to shower after ping-pong — and nothing bad had ever happened to me. And the water back then, gathered in the well when it rained or purchased from the water owner and his tanker trucks, was very different from the water here and didn't crystallize you outside and in, all the way to your core, nor did it steal your smell or change your way of being.

My mental trick worked as well as before, and I made it to the shower without being seen, and before my neighbor arrived in the adjoining bathroom, as he did every morning, I covered myself in ointment and petroleum jelly and let the water run without wetting me. Then I got dressed and sat down to wait for the others to get up and come to breakfast. They were surprised to see me awake already, but at the same time it's not as if I'd killed anyone; each person has the right to wake up the way they choose, so I suppose they didn't pay it too much mind.

At work, however, things got complicated. When our day was done, I tried not to go to the collective showers, but I ran into the supervisor. I told him I didn't feel well and might be getting sick, and he told me that he'd take me to the doctor as soon as I finished my shower. I told him I preferred to go home in hopes that rest might take care of it, and he said that was fine, as soon as I showered I could go home. Then I told him that just for this one day I'd rather shower when I got home, and he said that was perfect, as soon as I'd showered I could go shower at home. Since the conversation was becoming futile, I showered.

As I did so, the supervisor watched me through the glass wall.

That night I slept splendidly, without a single trace of worry, without thinking about my sons or about anything at all. Even so, the following day I made another attempt.

As I said, it wasn't hard to escape the shower at home, so my effort went into evading it at work. The only thing I could think of was to apply a thick layer of ointment on my naked body, so the water wouldn't enter my pores easily and wouldn't do whatever it had been doing.

After work, I parked my little worm of excrement and casually headed to the shower. To avoid raising my supervisor's suspicions, once there I tried to spend as little time as possible under the water and to pretend that I was getting wetter than I was, keeping my head out of the stream and talking nonstop with my coworkers, to conceal, as best I could, my true and sinister intentions. Of course I didn't drink any running water all day, as there was no point in avoiding the shower only to then let myself be crystallized from the inside, so when I finally arrived at the bar, I drank my first beer dying of thirst and my second beer dying of fear at the possibility of losing the little progress I'd made. One can suppose that the beer was also made from the same water, but I had to drink something if I didn't want to die, and if I had to drink something, it might as well be cold beer.

Despite the water I'd downed with my two or three or maybe it was four beers, that night I was able to observe the first effects of my diabolical plan. Rather than falling asleep completely happy, I fell asleep only halfway happy and was able to recall my children and miss them a little. I was glad not to be so glad, and I thought that if I repeated the whole operation each day, I might finally manage to not be happy at all and, what's more, in the best possible future, finally get really and truly pissed off. I fell asleep embracing my growing dissatisfaction, though I'll admit that I didn't rule out the possibility that I was going insane.

THE NEXT DAY, I HEWED TO MY NEW ROUTINE LIKE A NUT to its bolt: ointment, lies, half-showers, and a lot of beer. No trace of the former zone agent at the bar. That night, though, was even better than the one before. During dinner I felt the urge to strangle the young tutor, not an uncontrollable urge, it was too soon for that, but let's say the idea crossed my mind.

Julio's smile, before he fell asleep, consoled me of all my misfortunes. Under my eye mask, ferocious nightmares,

and they were welcome. That's how it was all week, until Friday. On Friday I decided at my own risk not to show
up for work. It was the first time I did that without being
ill, without a signed doctor's note in hand. I thought they
might arrest me on the street, that they might call her,
that they'd come in search of me, that they'd mobilize the
secret police — there was no other kind — but to my surprise none of that happened. I stood in front of the recycling and waste management center, and, after a few seconds of hesitation, I passed it and kept going. As I went, I
realized that I'd never walked in the city without having
somewhere to go, and I also realized that I didn't know this
city. Of course I knew my section of it — the recycling center, the bar, the sports center, the identical and transparent buildings that surrounded each of my familiar places
and the places that she or her lover chose for our rare
moments of leisure, the nearby movie theater that only
screened old musicals from long before the war, my section's park, my section's public library — but I'd never ven-
tured outside my section. In the years I'd spent inside, it
had never occurred to me to roam, just like that, until I'd
seen it all. Walk all the way to the border — if it had one —
of this strange crystallized city.

That morning, which was just like any other morning
for everyone else but which for me was different because
I'd decided that it was, I set out. And without thinking too
much about it.

I suppose the water in the showers had something to do with that, too, because once you were crystallized you lost your urge to do things just because you felt like it, on a whim. In fact, I couldn't remember the last time I'd come up with a plan on my own, other than my few escapades to the bar, although that, I'm afraid, isn't much to take heart in. Men, here and anywhere else in the world, tend to seek solace in beer at the end of a workday, and that doesn't exactly set them free. So I took a long walk through the city that beautiful and identical Friday morning, without an explanation that could justify my behavior in any way. I felt like I was turning a heavy ship around in the middle of a long voyage, disregarding the route marked on the map.

❖

What a large city, how it shone, how monotonous it was, how boring. My walk could not have been more different from my expectations. Section after section there was nothing but the same, street after street, warehouse after warehouse, bar after bar, movie theater after movie theater, all with the same old musicals I'd already seen a hundred times. No matter which direction you went, you arrived at one of its borders, from which you could see, through the walls of the transparent dome, the rest of the world, close and yet impossibly distant, and you could go for hours that way without discovering anything new in the city or its borders. I went this way and that, without seeing anything that surprised me, until by accident, as it was easy to get disoriented in all those repetitive neighborhoods, I found myself at the main gate, the one through which we'd arrived after abandoning our home. Beside the gate, just as I recalled it, stood the arrival camp. Through the large transparent tent I saw the miserable wretches who, like us so long ago, were starting their lives in this new world without the slightest suspicion of what awaited them, happy to be alive and sad to be so far from home, and I also saw those who ran the camp, as polite and cold as before, and two dead people hanging from a post beside the checkpoint. Two dead people I didn't know, two among the many who would never set foot under the crystal dome, doubtlessly condemned for their crimes during the war, for their treason, for their attachment to the old earth or their distrust toward this transparent life.

I couldn't help but approach, and as I did so, as if he'd been expecting me, my old friend the former zone agent came out to meet me. First, of course, a strong embrace, and what are you doing around here, and all the chitchat of false friendship, and although, why deny it, by this point I'd already fallen prey to the deepest distrust, my work had

worn me down and maybe for that reason I let myself tell
the truth.

When he asked me where I was headed, I replied that I
was going to see my sons, when he told me they weren't
here, I replied that I didn't believe him, when he called the
guards, I told them they'd have to kill me to stop me, when
they finally raised their fists, I stopped.

Sometimes a man says such things — *You'd have to kill me to
stop me* — to gather his courage and without giving it much
thought, and when he does give it thought, it's already too
late.

Surrender! all those men said together, and I have to admit that when I saw all those fists I lost my courage and
gave in. I fell to my knees and lowered my arms, and that
was when they descended on me.

Two blows knocked me down from my knees, blows that
stabbed my ribs like burning arrows. There's no ointment
to protect you from such blows. I prayed badly and very
fast, the only shred I remembered of a childhood prayer,
and I gave myself up for dead. *I'm dead!* I thought, but then
realized I was thinking this over and over again and understood that I was still alive. I was dying, or so it seemed to
me, and I recall that the former zone agent, merciful as he
was, tried to raise my spirits during what I thought was my
last breath by telling me that joke one more time about
the horse who's a lawyer and who screws some poor man's
wife, but this time I passed out before he made it to the end.

I didn't pass out the way I imagine dead people do, because my head spun with images and songs, familiar landscapes and all kinds of animals of a thousand colors like the ones I always looked at in Julio's book. I don't know whether the dead still dream, but I don't think so. So in my dream, and thanks to my dream, I could be sure that I wasn't dead.

THEY SAY THAT AFTER THE TURMOIL, I SLEPT FOR OVER two months.

It's possible, I don't know. It's hard to measure the time that goes by while you're asleep, but still, it didn't seem like that much to me. In fact, I only remember one dream, though it was a very long one.

In my dream, I was burying my two shotguns again, and carefully marking the spot with a stone, and then I was with the boy Julio, dousing the old house with gasoline, and we watched it burn down to its foundation, and then we were being taken on a bus, and a fighter-bomber attacked the line of buses and destroyed the one right behind ours, killing everyone, or so it seemed, because we barely dared to look, and soon after that our bus got a flat and we took refuge in a hotel with the water owners, and they abandoned us, taking the canteen with them, and we arrived at the crystal city and, in the end, the whole thing went on and on exactly as I've told it until, beside the arrival camp, where I'd gone with the wholesome goal of asking about my sons, the guards pounded me, and I thought I'd die but didn't die, and in a coma or between dreams I told this whole story. That is, in my dream, in that dream, the only thing that happened was me telling everything that had taken place. But to whom? To Julio. And the boy Julio, who was almost a man by now, sat by my side and listened without saying a word, but I could see in his eyes that he understood everything.

❖

When I woke, the hospital room was empty. Just a few flowers in a crystal vase beside the bed, lit by the midday sun. For a second I thought everything must have been a nightmare in which I was recounting that very same nightmare, until

I leaned toward the flowers and realized that they smelled of nothing, until I saw that the light was the same constant yellow light of the crystal city, until I saw the adjoining rooms through the transparent walls, and the rooms below me through the transparent floor, and the ones above through the transparent ceiling. With my hands, I felt the bandages over my ribs, which were surely broken, and felt the pain of the blows again. That, at the very least, was real. Scum! To beat me so brutally when I'd already surrendered. Who would do such a thing? I only wanted to learn something about my sons, and maybe a thing or two about this damn city. It's not so much to ask. I didn't find out anything about my sons, but I did get clear, once and for all, what these people are really about. I've been warned. It's always the same, all pretty words until you want to do something for yourself, and then the problems start. This place is a living hell, and yet nobody seems to realize it. Why did I realize it? Am I some kind of sick man, have I lost my patience, am I so attached to my own ways that I can't manage to forget them? Why does it suffocate me to see everyone around me, to never stop seeing them, not even in my own home, nor here in a hospital room, why am I irritated by their presence through the glass? Why is it so hard for me to bear that it never gets dark, that there's nowhere to hide? Am I a traitor to the collective cause? And if so, why haven't they hung me face-down, once and for all, as they did with the water owners? Why wound me with-

out killing me? As I asked myself these questions, it dawned
on me that I was actually seeking a different answer. How
do the others bear it? Is it enough for them to put food on
your plate for you to put up with everything? True, I had
never seen anyone go hungry here, and there was always
a doctor at the ready to cure what ailed us, and there were
no bosses, no force, no command, and because of the water or whatever it was you felt protected and happy, even
against your own will, but was that enough to live? Why
did I miss the blood of animals I'd shot down in the forest?
Why did I actively seek out this punishment and not let up
until I found it, and why was I touching the sore surface of
my wounds beneath my bandages as if stroking treasure?
What kind of madman am I that when I think of them,
all of the people around me, I feel nothing but the deepest
scorn? Why don't I feel the same scorn for myself? Where
does it come from, this strange fondness I have for myself,
when I'm neither different from nor better than the rest of
my absurd fellow city dwellers?

The old days weren't perfect either, I didn't live the best
of lives, but back then not even war or fear could poison
me like this perpetual well-being did. And I loved her then
without giving it any thought, and now, since we'd arrived
here, to be precise, I see her as an enemy or a stranger. It's
not that I came to think of her differently, it's that she's
changed toward me. If I can't blame her, it's because I don't
know for certain whether to trust the truth of my own

eyes or the truth that doubtlessly exists on the other side, and because my eyes, from so much seeing without questioning, no longer know how to calibrate trust. There's nothing about her to justify my betrayal or the betrayal I've surely committed by letting her grow away from me without putting up any resistance, without protest, without a peep.

Nor did my dawn-to-dusk labor on the land ever disgust me as my job here does, without ever varying, something to do and little else, and the people of our town for whom I felt no affection nevertheless did not repulse me like the people of this city, and I wasn't wary of the water, nor did it ever cross my mind that it could be rotting me from the inside, and I even paid for water when rain wouldn't fall and never complained about the price, and that's how I paid for everything, more than it was worth, without complaining, and I accepted the bombs and the shadow of death falling over my own family without thinking for an instant of rebelling. Nor was I attached to my country, nor was I a patriot, nor did I hate enemy nations, indifferent as I was to their fate. This is all to say, there in my other life I was a nobody, I didn't care much about other people's misfortune, I didn't feel part of anything beyond the forest and the land and my own home and family. Only she, Augusto, and Pablo truly mattered to me, until that boy wandered out of the forest alone and infiltrated the tiny circle of my affections and concerns.

Whereas here, in this place where I'm part of something functional that assures my well-being and calls for my participation, I feel inexorably excluded from the common good. What malice lurks in the soul of a man who won't recognize himself as one among many? It's hard to understand that this place has changed me so much. It's hard to blame the transparent city for all my troubles. A man should be able to travel from one place to another without losing his soul. I don't know for sure anymore whether the man I am now — constantly poisoning the happiness that surrounds me — is the result of our transfer here, or whether I was always like this and it's only here that I've come to see it. Maybe I deserve everything that's happened to me, and that's why I enjoy my wounds more than I did the health I was given. Maybe I brought the trouble with me and these people are entirely innocent. It's hard for me to believe, but it could be. Ever since I was a kid I've been slow to trust, it never seemed that life gave enough to go around sharing, only with her did I enjoy some intimacy, the kind that's normal between two people married before God, and together we cared for our land and our sons, but I didn't open my heart to her — why did I have to? It's not as if I had reason to think there was much inside. Nor did I hide much worth writing home about, there were no secrets. She and I loved each other the way people do, without giving it too much thought, until the war began, and maybe during the war we loved each other even more, or at least that's how it was for me, probably because there were bombs and threats outside, and because we both felt the same fear of never seeing our children again, and then later, in the strange peace of the transparent city, little by little we came to not love each other at all. It could be because we weren't allowed to smell each other, although, if we're something more than animals, and I hope we are, it can't only be that.

To be honest, I wasn't aware back then of being more or less than what I am now, and in none of my other lives —as a boy, as a laborer, as a foreman, as an owner, as a lover—was I anything else, nor do I see myself as different enough to warrant panic in this new life as an exile or a prisoner or whatever I am. And if this is the little I have now, the wounds caused by blows to my ribs and a few memories, I suppose that it's the little I've earned, and in truth I've never had much more, so, really, why complain? I won't be the one to shout at the heavens.

⁘

And that's what I was thinking about—accepting the sentence I had imposed upon myself without blaming anybody else and, therefore, forgiving these good people for the way they treated me—when Julio came in and pulled

up a glass chair and sat down beside me and, to my astonishment, began to talk.

"How are you, Father?"

Before I answered, I realized two things: these were the
first words I'd ever heard Julio speak, and this was the first
voice I'd heard outside my own head for a long time.

"Fine," I answered, without knowing whether it was
true.

"Don't be too worried, it's harder for some people to accept than others."

"Accept what?"

"The adaptation. That's why they brought us here, so
we could start to accept the idea of adapting, but some
people can't deal with it."

"Since when can you talk?"

"Since you've been here. After your accident, I had no
choice but to talk. Without you in the house, someone had
to take care of the family."

"What about that other guy? Your tutor?"

"He's an idiot."

"I knew it! And by the way, I don't know what they've
told you, but it was no accident. I was beaten up."

"I know. But that's what they call it."

"Who is 'they'?"

"They, all of them. Here nobody is different or better
than anyone else, nobody's in charge, everything is orga-

nized by us collectively. There isn't anyone who tells us anything, we all tell each other."

"I've never been in charge of anything, nor have I organized much, nor have I said anything very important . . ."

"Nobody does, that's the trick, that way there's no one to blame. In this city there's no authority, no complaint to make or anyone to take it to, nothing to fight for or explain, no one to fight or explain things to . . ."

"What about the provisional government?"

"The provisional government is us, everyone we see through the walls. Those people who vote at union meetings. All of us, every one of us."

"They were right at your school. You sure are bright."

"Thank you, Father."

"I've been dreaming about you. I dreamed that you were sitting right here and I was telling you a story."

"You've told it to me."

"Then I wasn't dreaming."

"Yes, you were dreaming, but you talked in your sleep. And I was listening."

"Did anyone else hear me raving?"

"No, just me."

"And whose side are you on?"

"The same as always: our side."

"And which side is that?"

"The one for people who are going to get out of here

and return to the old region, and go up the hill and into the forest to dig out two shotguns. The one for people who haven't yet surrendered. And now, try to rest, because I need you strong. We're leaving."

"What about her?"

"She'll stay, she likes this. Mother thinks you've failed her, that you've fallen apart, that you don't want to improve."

"I don't blame her."

"She's made her decision, she's free to make it. We should make ours."

"I made mine a long time ago, then I forgot about it, but now all of a sudden I remember it clearly. When the hell are we getting out of here?"

"Tomorrow."

"Perfect. How?"

"In your shit worm, Father. I've stolen it from the garage in the shit recycling center and I've hidden it in the grass just beyond the transparent wall."

"And nobody saw?"

"Nobody sees anything here."

"They saw me, and they beat me."

"You went head-on, Father, and that's no way to go about it, you have to attack from the side."

"Now I get it — from the side. One more thing, that shit worm I used to drive, you may have noticed it isn't very fast. You really think we can use it to escape? Maybe if we unhook the containers full of shit . . ."

"No, the shit is essential."

"For —?"

"For throwing them off our trail. I've got everything ready, don't worry, you just rest, I'll come for you in the morning."

"It sounds too easy. It won't go well."

"It's even easier than you think, Father, and it'll go fine. Nobody really wants to leave here, and it's not even forbidden. So everything is poorly guarded."

"If it's not forbidden, why don't we leave through the main gate, fair and square?"

"Just in case."

"Oh . . ."

After that, I fell silent. It was clear that the kid was much smarter than me, and there was no point in doubting his ideas or trying to line them up with mine.

Julio kissed me on the forehead and left. I watched him go, confident and sure of himself, a man. Through the walls I watched him walk, just as I'd once watched my real sons go into the forest on their way to war. He wasn't my son, but I'd cared for him as if he were, and he called me Father and everything, and in any case he was all I had left. I have to admit that I felt awfully proud.

The excitement of our upcoming escape made it hard

to sleep. I closed my eyes and tried to recall the exact place where I'd hidden my guns; as always happens when you need it, my memory didn't fail. It was like walking on our land again, each tree in the forest present and alive, and the scent of fresh moss and the small pools and the rustle of weasels hidden beneath branches flooded my senses, and in the deepest part of the forest where the pines barely let in light, I saw the rock that marked my hiding place. The forest was the same as in my memory, and this made me calm, but not like before, when I couldn't help but feel that way. This was a different calm, the kind that comes when you understand the threat but feel protected from it.

I WOKE UP EARLY, THOUGH IT WAS IMPOSSIBLE TO KNOW the exact time. In this place where daylight never changed, it was hard to know when things took place, how much effort each person put into things, how patient or rushed you should be. Urgency was lost in this constant, sinister light.

The sick people around me were still sleeping in their eye masks. I stood up and waited for Julio to come.

I waited and waited without knowing for how long.

Nurses came in with food, followed by a couple of doctors, who gave too many explanations about my delicate condition that I didn't remotely understand. I wasn't really paying attention, to be honest, and wasn't sure that those were the right words for having had the crap beaten out of me, but of course I'm no doctor. I think one of them said that I'd gone mad, that the hospital's walls were actually made of concrete, that the city wasn't crystal or glass at all. That everything still had its odors, above all me, as I refused to shower. They also told me that Julio didn't speak, and that he was no exceptionally gifted child but rather developmentally delayed, and that this was why he'd been removed from school, and that the man who lived in my home looked after him because I was not considered equipped to care for anyone, and that my other sons, the real ones, had disappeared in combat and had been given up for dead. They said all of this to me in a very serious tone and without hesitating for a second, which was how I knew they were lying.

I wasn't offended, though I knew none of it was true; I didn't even care, I'm not one to pay strangers any mind, no matter how educated they might be.

When all those strangers entered the room I got into bed, and when they left I stood back up and waited.

I waited—standing there in my glass room, for days, surrounded by sick people lying in their beds—for Julio, who was now a grown man, to come for me.

❖

But he never came.

❖

Not so much as a note, not a signal, nothing.

I guessed that he'd been captured. Maybe he wasn't so bright after all. Perhaps he'd tricked me, who knows, though he didn't seem the type. I preferred to think that these people, who seem to decide things on their own, had decided to finish him off. Or he was even brighter than I thought and he'd set off without me. I'd never blame him for that, he was young and strong and had his whole life ahead of him. Why should he carry the dead weight of an old man? It almost made me happy to think he might have abandoned me. I'd be of little help to him out there.

I pictured him mounting my little shit tractor with the shit worm hooked up behind it, advancing slowly but firmly toward a better life. What Julio would never be able to find, no matter how bright he was, were my shotguns, because I'm the one who buried them and only I can find them.

JULIO WASN'T COMING AND THAT WAS PROBABLY BEST for him, the most sensible thing.

It made me sad to think I might not see him again, but I was still happy, convinced that he'd never come back for me. How could I ask such a special young man, with so much to discover on his own in this godly world, to drag his old father along on his adventures, and not even his real father, but his almost-father, who would be nothing more than a dead weight, a burden, a terrible bother?

If he wanted to save himself, the poor kid had no choice
but to cast me off along the way.

❖

I kept standing in wait, just in case.

❖

One day, she came with a lawyer and I don't know how
many divorce papers and other, more confusing documents that would give her full custody of Julio. As soon
as I saw them approaching, I got into bed and put on my
best sick-patient face. I told them that I didn't care about
the divorce, but when it came to Julio they could forget it.
I told them that Julio had fled without looking back, he
was already gone from this stupid city and its ridiculous
laws thanks to his vast intelligence, and those papers full
of small print made me laugh, because the boy they were
trying to gain custody of was already a free man on a flight
of his own.

They said no, that Julio wasn't flying, that Julio didn't

even talk, that poor Julio was as calm today as he was every day, at his special school for the developmentally delayed.

If they'd pierced my soul with a spear they couldn't have hurt me more. So it seemed that according to these idiots the boy wasn't a genius. I wasn't prepared to believe that, not for anything in the world. In any case, it seemed to me that the most urgent matter in that moment was to get rid of them.

I signed the papers without protest and they left immediately. People leave very quickly once they have what they want.

And of course, as soon as they were gone I stood up again.

And I kept waiting.

And I waited so long, in my pajamas, that time stretched out and a lot of it passed, and then I waited a little longer, because you never know. When it came to patience, fate couldn't hold a candle to me, nor could the devil.

❖

In short, I waited a very long time and for nothing, and in the end I had no choice but to start devising my own escape, alone, without anyone's help. Trusting in my own intelligence, my own instinct, and my own fortune.

❖

I'd be lying if I said it didn't cross my mind to surrender.

LEAVING THE TRANSPARENT CITY WASN'T AS HARD AS I'D imagined, there was no need for a plan, all I had to do was gather the courage I had left until I was ready, like scraping crumbs off the ground and mashing them together in your hands until they look somewhat like bread. So one fine day, with that small lump of courage in my arms, I walked in my pajamas, past distracted patients and nurses indifferent to my fate, all the way to the hospital doors, and I continued on the streets that separated me from the city gate, past the arrival camp and then the checkpoint, without any opposition whatsoever. I suppose that when they saw how firm I was, how determined, and how unusually dressed, they took me for a madman. What I can't understand now is why they beat me when I asked about my sons and then, later, let me leave without opposition, it must be that in the crystal city people were highly bothered by questions but not at all upset by escapes. I don't think what I did can even be called an escape, this openly leaving a place where no one and nothing is forcing you to stay. In any case, I walked out as calm as can be and circled the perimeter of the dome without any trouble from the guards, and I searched the undergrowth for the little tractor Julio said he'd hidden, but it wasn't there, I don't know why, whether it was because the kid didn't want to help me or because he couldn't, it didn't matter, it wasn't really his problem whether his almost-father wanted to be inside or out, near or far, so without holding anything against the boy — what fault could he have, the little angel? — I went back to the highway and walked straight to the field and from there to the mountain until I was very far away, and I kept walking and walking and leaving more and more land behind me. And finally I arrived at the only logical conclusion: I'd dreamed my conversation with him. I had no doubt about it anymore, the boy couldn't talk. And if he did talk one day, God willing, it wouldn't be with me.

❖

Three days later, I'd reached our region. On the way, I hadn't bumped into anyone, and one could say that I'd been lucky. Instead of going the same way I'd come, I decided to follow my intuition and go around the mountain, disregarding the highway we'd walked on when we traveled together, she, Julio, and I. When it came down to it, the last thing I wanted was to run into anyone.

I had nothing with me. The first night I slept out in the open, without food or water. On the second day I found an enormous garbage dump where I foraged all the essentials for my journey: not only warm clothes, but also a large piece of tarp with which I could build a tent, blankets, empty bottles that I filled with murky water from a puddle, and boots missing their laces but whose soles were in decent condition, no holes, and they were almost my size. The good boots of a dead soldier, like the ones my sons wore in that war. I found nothing to eat except plants and berries, arbutus and juniper, but it was enough. The clothes I put on — pants torn at the knees and a wool sweater in pretty good shape — stank, but given that I was sick and tired of not being able to smell anything all those years in the city, I must admit I was grateful for the stench. I felt accompanied by the sweat of those who'd worn these clothes before me, and though it wasn't yet my own, that borrowed odor was familiar in a lost, distant way.

On the third night, it rained, and I was able to exchange the puddle water in my bottles for clean rainwater that tasted like glory. When I woke the next day, I could see my region in the distance, and the joy it gave me to recognize the contours of what had been my land would be hard to imagine if you've never been forced from your home, and easy to understand for anyone who's been exiled. I set out very early and soon reached the town, or what was left of it. Nobody came out to greet me, as there was no one left, not a soul. No men, no rats, no dogs. Weeds grew in the streets and between the charred stones of houses. The stores, the bar, the post office, all of it burned and in ruins. The ground covered in broken glass, the church still almost in one piece but blackened, the public pool full of stagnant, putrid water. The fountains silent. The bell tower was missing its bell, God knows why, maybe they'd melted it for cannonballs or bronze coins. I walked through the town without seeing a single animal or insect or ghost, nothing remotely alive or dead, and headed toward my land. I saw the house burned down to its foundation, the wild garden that no longer looked any different from the surrounding land, the barren orchard, the empty stables, the dry wells. Nothing of ours had survived. I consoled my-

self by passing what was no longer my home and putting
it behind me until I reached the forest. At least the forest
was still what it had been before. I searched for the rock
that marked the place where I'd hidden my weapons, but
I couldn't find it. Floods and bombs had changed the terrain, or perhaps my memory failed me, or someone else
had dug them out and they weren't my guns anymore.
Maybe I'd been a fool to think I'd find my own mark before others did. I dug with my hands here and there, like
a mole, without success, until I sat down in exhaustion to
rest under a tree as night began to fall. For an instant, I
missed the crystal city, my transparent walls and ceiling,
and I missed her, the boy Julio, the little I'd had there,
but I decided with more rancor than enthusiasm that I'd
never return. I'd never go back, and never again would I
long for my past captivity. I swore never to set foot in the
transparent city again. Not to see everyone else if I could
avoid it, nor let others be condemned to see me. I also decided that, should I ever encounter anyone, I'd warmly
greet only those who, like me, were able to hide.

I swore to live here, in the forest, for whatever life I had
left, and to die here when the time came. Alone or accompanied, that remained to be seen.

I looked for thick branches and built my tent. The place
that, from this moment on, would be my home. Under the
tarp, surrounded by the deepest darkness, alone and per-

manently disarmed, I felt the renewed stirring of my old, healthy, and longed-for optimism.

Familiar voices shrouded that strange moment before sleep, imagined or remembered, but, in the end, known to me. Voices that knew nothing of collapse, displacement, and defeat.

Finally close to the only victory, or at least to the recollection of my voice, the one that had been with me — and only me — since I was a boy, before everything and everyone else.

❖

I don't know how long I slept, nor do I remember what I dreamed, but when I woke the sun was high, and when I stood, as I stretched, I thought I saw a man in the distance. Without thinking, I grabbed a stick and waited to see whether he was coming in my direction. And soon I saw that he was, in fact, headed directly toward me. But that wasn't what worried me most, the worst part was that, little by little, as he approached, his figure started seeming vaguely familiar, and then very familiar, and after a while I knew for sure that it was Julio.

This must have been the way she saw him arrive that

first day, only now he was bigger and not wounded, not defenseless, but armed.

He was carrying a crossbow, the kind that could kill a wild boar from three hundred meters away and hit a moving target, and there I was, still as a post from surprise, and maybe also out of joy.

I cast the stick aside, because no matter what happened, I had no intention of hitting Julio, and to be honest I couldn't have bested him anyway, crossbow or no. So I sat there and waited like a man who's accepted his destiny, come what may, and the closer he got, without knowing why — intuition, I imagine — the more certain I was that he was not bringing good news.

When he was two hundred meters away, he waved in greeting, and I responded, reflexively.

❖

Finally he arrived, and before saying a word he sat down, not beside me but in front of me. Without letting go of the crossbow, which he held firmly, his finger on the trigger. It sent shivers up my spine. When I met his gaze, I could barely see in this man the boy I'd wanted to make my own, who ran through the house dying of laughter, who so loved to draw exotic animals, who was without a doubt the only person whose company I could trust during those insufferable and transparent days in the crystal city.

I sensed that he wasn't here to join me, but to hunt me down.

Since I knew he wasn't going to say anything, I asked the relevant questions.

The following three:

Have you come here to take me back?

He shook his head.

Have you come here to kill me?

He nodded.

What am I accused of, exactly?

To this he did not reply, as is logical, so I reframed the question as best I could, in a manner that would let him answer without opening his mouth.

There won't be any more people like me in the world you're all building, right?

He nodded again, with the barest gesture, and I want to imagine that it was not without some pain.

Then he raised the crossbow to hip level, there was no need to raise it all the way when he had me so close.

At that moment I gave in, and as for the fate of the others in that new world, there's little I can tell. I imagine they'll do splendidly and that people like me, with no faith in the future, were always the enemy.

❖

One thing is certain. When it comes to me, they'd won.

❖

All I longed for — before it all clouded over, the visible and the invisible, the transparent and the most secret — was for my real sons to be on their side too, and not on mine.

❖

You have to know when your time has passed.

❖

And learn to admire other victories.